The camera still sat on the table beside her. Though he knew the photo would torture him, he couldn't help himself.

He picked it up and snapped a shot of Ivy and Gabe. They looked happy and peaceful.

Clearing his throat, Carter touched Ivy's arm to wake her. Her eyelids fluttered open and she smiled up at him. His heart pounded with the urge to kiss her lips.

"I couldn't have done this without you."

"I was glad to help."

She was. The truth of it always shone on her face. Carter wanted to care about her. Yearned for it. But he didn't deserve it.

He leaned down to take Gabe from her arms. His mouth came just shy of her head. The scent of her shampoo tickled his senses. Unable to stop himself, he allowed a slight kiss to the top of her head before he stood with Gabe in his arms. He had to get out of there.

JENNIFER JOHNSON

and her unbelievably supportive husband, Albert, are happily married and raising Brooke, Hayley, and Allie, the three cutest young ladies on the planet. Besides being a middle school teacher, Jennifer loves to read, write, and chauffeur her girls. She is a member of American Christian Fiction Writers. Blessed beyond measure, Jennifer hopes to always think like a child—bigger than imaginable and with complete faith. Send her a note at jenwrites4god@bellsouth.net.

Books by Jennifer Johnson

HEARTSONG PRESENTS

Pantry
Promises

Jennifer Johnson

Heartsong Presents

This story is dedicated to Minnie Cawby, a woman who pledged
her life to Jim and his three daughters. More than twenty years have
passed and she still loves those girls (and her own daughter) as well
as the grandchildren who've come along. This book is dedicated to
any woman who has accepted the challenge and privilege of raising
children who have lost their mother. May God bless you!

A note from the Author:

*I love to hear from my readers! You may correspond with
me by writing:*

**Jennifer Johnson
Author Relations
P.O. Box 9048
Buffalo, NY 14240-9048**

ISBN-13: 978-0-373-48624-3

PANTRY PROMISES

This edition issued by special arrangement with Barbour Publishing,
Inc., 1810 Barbour Drive, Uhrichsville, Ohio, U.S.A.

Copyright © 2012 by Jennifer Johnson

Scripture taken from the HOLY BIBLE, NEW INTERNATIONAL VERSION®. NIV®.
Copyright © 1973, 1978, 1984 by International Bible Society. Used by
permission of Zondervan. All rights reserved.

This is a work of fiction. Names, characters, places and incidents are
either the product of the author's imagination or are used fictitiously,
and any resemblance to actual persons, living or dead, business
establishments, events or locales is entirely coincidental.

PRINTED IN THE U.S.A.

Chapter 1

Carter Smith's heart pounded like a hammer striking a nail. Unclenching his fists, he sucked in a breath and begged God for strength not to wring his client's neck.

James spread his arms, holding an oversized soft drink in his right hand. "I'm sorry, Carter. I know I promised I'd get the money to you this week, but I just don't have it."

"You said that two weeks ago. And two weeks before that."

With fast-food bags in one hand, James's wife hustled past them with their elementary-school-aged, ballerina-decked-out daughter scurrying behind her. She opened the front door—the one Carter had installed—and slipped inside. Carter knew she walked on the hardwood floors he had laid. Took the fast-food dinner and placed it on the kitchen counter he had installed, surrounded by tile backsplash he had cemented. And yet, he had not seen the first penny in payment.

Carter's jaw twitched with the effort to hold back the biting words threatening to spill from his mouth. If he hadn't happened upon the family returning home, they would have ignored his knocks at the front door. Again.

"Two more weeks. I promise I'll get it to you."

Carter glanced back at the minivan in desperate need of a new set of tires. Lauren, his seven-year-old, was twisted in her seat talking to his youngest, Gabe. No doubt the three-year-old had grown bored waiting for Dad to return to the van. His five-year-old, Clay, looked out the window, probably searching the sky for airplanes—the child's favorite mode of transportation, though he'd never been on one.

Carter scrunched his eyes closed. He'd emptied his checking account into the mortgage payment and half tank of gas. He didn't have money for groceries. He turned back to James. "I need at least half. Today."

"Sorry. Can't do it." James shrugged and walked away.

Carter fell into step beside him. "You have to. You owe me."

James stopped at the front door. "Look. I know you need the money. But times are tough for all of us."

Carter thought of the fast-food dinner James and his family would enjoy, the dance lessons his daughter was obviously still able to attend. James had no conception of tough times. In two years' time, Carter had lost his wife and his business. He couldn't even feed his children, if this man didn't pay him something. Anything. It wasn't as if he asked for a handout. James had owed him for over a month.

James gripped the front doorknob. "You're just going to have to wait."

Carter balled his fists. Noting the rise in his blood pressure and acceleration of his heartbeat, he shoved his hands in his front pockets to keep from pummeling the man. "If needed, I will take you to court."

James opened the door and stepped inside. "Two weeks. I promise."

He shut the door before Carter could respond. Itching to beat down the door with his bare hands, Carter clenched his teeth and closed his eyes. After taking several deep breaths, he peered up at the heavens. "God, what am I gonna do?"

He looked back at the van. Gabe was crying. Lauren had obviously given up. She sat forward with her hands cupping her ears. Clay still looked at the window. Carter pinched his lips together. He worried about that boy. Since his mother's death, Clay lived in a fantasy world. He was a good, easy kid, but he didn't get upset at anything. Didn't show sadness or anger. Or happiness. Just seemed to have given up.

Making his way back to the van, Carter popped open the trunk, scooped a juice box out of a cooler, and handed it over the seat to his youngest child. Gabe sniffled then sucked on the straw.

"Dad, I'm hungry. It's past lunchtime." Lauren sounded much older than her seven years. Angry. Bitter. And put out with him.

"I know, sweetie. We'll head home now."

Carter jiggled the keys in his hand as he walked to the driver's side. What would he feed them? There were a couple cans of ravioli left. Yuck. The thought of eating that turned his stomach, but he believed there was still a bit of peanut butter. No bread, but he could eat some on crackers. There might still be a jar of peaches. The boys would like that, though Lauren would probably turn up her nose.

"He didn't pay you, did he?"

Lauren's words cut like a knife through his chest. He

pulled out of the driveway. She shouldn't know they were struggling. She should be thinking about baby dolls and dress up.

He looked at her in the rearview mirror. "No. He didn't. But that's not for you to worry about."

Back at home, he fixed the meager lunch for the kids. As he expected, Lauren frowned at the canned fruit, but she didn't say anything. Her silence was like a second jab in his heart. Shouldn't she complain and whine that she wanted something different? Shouldn't he have to fuss at her for not being appreciative for what they had? Instead, his little princess sat stoically beside her brothers, bitterness rolling off her like boiling water bubbling out of a pot.

Glancing away, he spied the pile of bills on the counter. He dotted a cracker with peanut butter as he thumbed through the mass. A knot caught in his throat when he saw the voucher Ms. Rolen had given him.

The sweet senior had been a bundle of nerves when she handed him the paper. Fumbled all over herself as she explained she knew he wouldn't want to use it but that God provided in various ways. It wounded his pride that his financial woes had been so obvious to his fellow church members.

He thumbed the corner of the voucher. The pantry closed in an hour. He'd never, in all thirty years of his life, taken a handout. He scanned the cupboard. Dinner tonight might be possible. He might even be able to scrounge up enough for breakfast, but after that, he was in trouble. And he had to provide for his children.

His stomach churned and his heartbeat raced at the thought of walking into a food pantry for help, not to leave a donation. *God, I don't know if I can do this.*

"You have too much pride to accept My provision?"

Carter swallowed back the knot in his throat. He cleared

the table and wiped Gabe's face. "Get your shoes on, kids. We're going to get groceries."

Ivy Adams arranged the last can of green beans on the shelf. She straightened the disheveled rows of corn then penciled in the vegetable to the list of items that were running low at the pantry. The bell jangled at the front, and Ivy stood and brushed her hands against her jeans. "Coming."

Plastering a smile on her lips, she pushed aside the disappointment that this would most likely be the last customer she'd have until Christmas break. She enjoyed volunteering at the food pantry, but with school starting in a little over a week, she'd soon spend her days with second graders instead. She loved teaching. Wouldn't change professions for anything, but every fall she missed her time at the food pantry as well. She'd still stock shelves on Saturdays, but she wouldn't get to shop with the people—which was where she felt the most joy.

She squirted some hand sanitizer in her hand then rounded the corner and stopped. A dark-haired man was bent down tying a young boy's shoe. Another boy, a few years older, stood beside him with his legs crossed, bouncing on his toes. The girl, who looked to be the same age as Ivy's students, jutted her thumb toward her brother. "He's gotta go to the bathroom."

The man looked up. His deep brown eyes, kind and gentle, drew her. When he stood to his full height, Ivy bit her bottom lip at the sight of the span of his chest.

"I'm sorry." He pointed to his son. "Do you have a restroom we could use?"

Ivy blinked to regain her senses. "Sure." She motioned him forward. "Follow me."

Once the man and his kids had shut the door behind them, Ivy raked her fingers through her hair. She fiddled with her shirt collar then pulled on the hem to flatten out any wrinkles. She shook her head. *Get a grip, Ivy. He's just a customer. Nothing more.*

She inhaled a deep breath. It had been a long day. And this was always an emotional one for her, since it was her last for a few months. She was just being sentimental.

The door opened and three children exited and then the man. Ivy felt her face heat up. Good looking didn't cut it. She hadn't thought the word since college, but the man was *smokin' hot* with a double *T*, as she and her sister used to say.

She bit back a chuckle as she clapped her hands. "So, how can I help you?"

He shoved a voucher toward her. Ivy noted red streaking up his neck. The size of his chest and arms were proof physical labor wasn't foreign to him. He and his children wore clean, trendy clothing. This was obviously something he wasn't used to doing. She knew a lot of families had taken a hit with the plummeting economy. They were obviously one of them.

She took the paper and motioned for them to follow her back to the front of the building. She opened the record book. "May I have your name and address?"

"Why?"

"We have to keep a record of everyone who comes. And I will need to see a form of ID."

"Why?"

Ivy looked up into his eyes. Embarrassment and pride mingled in the dark orbs. She'd helped many people who struggled with accepting assistance, and she could tell this man would have battled a grizzly to avoid getting help now. She'd probably never see him again, but she had to follow protocol.

She placed the pen on the pad and cupped her hands

together. "The truth is there are people who would take advantage of coming here. They would show up more than once a week, any time someone different is volunteering. We want to provide for as many people as possible—"

"I would never do that."

"I can tell that's true, but—"

"I can't do this." The man scooped the youngest boy in his arms and grabbed the older boy's hand.

"Wait." Ivy grabbed his arm then gasped at the strength of his bicep. He peered back at her, and she swallowed. What was she thinking grabbing the man's arm? A tingle shimmied through her. She'd never felt such a large muscle.

She cleared her throat. Realizing she still held his arm, she jerked back her hand. "You're not a guy who accepts help. I can see that. But you must have come here for a reason."

"Come on, kids." The man turned and nudged the girl and older boy toward the door.

"Wait." She had no idea why she was trying so hard to get the man to stay. Something about him and the little one he had tended to so closely. Something about the blond boy who'd had to go to the bathroom. The girl who looked at Ivy as if she wanted to give her a piece of her mind. The whole family drew her in like a challenging sudoku puzzle. Once she started, she had to see it through.

She walked around in front of them and placed her hand on her chest. Peering into his dark eyes, she feared she'd lose herself in their abyss. "Look. I'm Ivy. I live in Ridgeview. See, that wasn't so hard."

She swallowed and blinked her way back to reality. She'd just given a complete stranger the gist of her address.

"You give complete strangers your address?"

She furrowed her brows. "Not usually. My mom would be mortified."

A slow smile lifted his lips. "Okay. I'll swallow my pride. I'd been praying to push it back anyway."

Praying? She churned his words around in her mind. Maybe he was a Christian. The kindness she'd seen in his eyes when he first looked up at her would suggest it.

He released his son's hand and pulled his wallet from his back pocket. "Name's Carter Smith." He flipped open the wallet. "And here's my address."

She walked around him and grabbed the pad and pen from the table. Her hands shook as she jotted down his information. Glancing up at him, she noted his smirk. She shook her hand and forced a laugh. "Too much caffeine. Makes me shaky."

He nodded, and she wanted to crawl under the table and hide. *What is wrong with me? I have got to get a grip. The guy has three kids, which means he probably has a wife at home.*

She bit the inside of her lip. Which made her wonder why his wife hadn't come. She rarely had families with only the father and kids. Almost always she helped a mother and her kids or a mother and father with their kids. Unless the guy was a single father.

As he placed his youngest son in a shopping cart, she peeked at his left ring finger. No wedding band. *He must not be married.* She inwardly scolded herself. *The man obviously works in manual labor. He may not wear a band for safety reasons.* If the guy was married, it was downright disturbing that she was allowing butterfly fluttering over a husband and father.

"Just stop it," she mumbled to herself.

Carter started to pull the boy out of the seat. "I'm sorry."

"No, no." Ivy waved her hands. "I'm sorry. I was thinking out loud. He can sit there. Let me clean it first." She pulled a disinfectant wipe from its container, wiped off the front bar, then tossed the wipe.

He secured the boy in the seat, and Ivy took in a long breath. Forcing herself to remain professional, she guided them through the pantry. Never before had she acted so disoriented. She'd nearly passed out at the sight of him then offered up her name and address to get him to stay. *Why don't I just go ahead and ask him on a date while I'm at it? I'm sure his wife would enjoy that—if he has one.*

Heat rushed up her neck and cheeks. If he looked at her, he'd wonder why she was blushing. Thankfully, he was preoccupied with the boys as they debated two flavors of cereal. She looked at his daughter. She seemed so unhappy. Ivy wanted to wrap the girl in a hug, but Carter hadn't offered the children's names and she wasn't sure if she should ask.

They finished the trek through the pantry, and Ivy helped the family out to their minivan. With the groceries loaded in the back, she grabbed the cart with one hand and waved to the family with the other.

"Dad, does she look like my mom?"

Carter shut the door, and Ivy pretended not to hear the question as she made her way back into the pantry. They didn't know their mother? She wondered what had happened to her. Were they divorced? Had she passed away?

Her heart constricted anew for the children. They were so young. They needed a mom's hugs and kisses. She thought of the sadness behind the girl's eyes. She needed a woman in her life.

She opened the door and pushed the cart into its place. The back door opened, and Brent Connors walked in. His eyes twinkled with his smile, and Ivy couldn't help but smile in return.

"How'd your last day go?"

He made his way toward her then wrapped her up in a hug. He smelled good, and his hugs were always warm and genuine. Her mother had picked Brent as Ivy's future mate, but Ivy didn't see him that way. She was thankful he seemed to share her feelings. He better fit the part of the brother-she'd-never-had-but-would-have-adored.

Letting her go, he grabbed the pad off the front table. "Let's go add today's customers into the computer system and check inventory."

She nodded and followed him back to the small office. They finished the work then Brent shut down the computer. "How 'bout I treat you to dinner in celebration of another great summer?"

Ivy took in Brent's wavy sandy hair and deep blue eyes. She didn't want to lead him on. He was a terrific man. Christian counselor at one of the pro-life centers in town. Volunteer director at the food pantry. And absolutely adorable. He would make someone a great husband, and sometimes she wished she felt what her mother wanted.

He winked and flicked her in the arm. "Come on. I know you're hungry."

She crinkled her nose and flicked him back. "Okay. But for that, I'm buying the most expensive thing on the menu."

Brent laughed, and Ivy grabbed her purse from the desk's drawer. What could it hurt to let him take her to dinner? Simply friends. Nothing more.

Chapter 2

"Arthritis acting up?" Ivy watched her mother rub her hands together from across the table.

Mom released a sigh and sat back against the booth. "Ten-hour shifts may be a bit long for me."

Ivy wished her mom would go ahead and retire from her nursing position at the hospital. But Mom wouldn't do it. She needed two more years to get the retirement percentage she needed, and she enjoyed helping people too much.

"Not to worry." Mom picked up a menu. "I'll soak in a hot bath when we get home."

"Sorry we're late."

Ivy turned and saw her adopted sister, Mirela, and husband, Josif, approaching the booth with Bella and Benny. Mirela pointed to the toddler while pinching her nose with her index finger and thumb like a clothespin. "Benny honored us with a little present that we had to take care of just as we were about to walk out the door."

Mom shimmied out of the booth and swooped the boy into her arms. Her strength always renewed at the sight of the kids.

Bella scooted beside Ivy in the booth and splayed her fingers against the table. "Look what Josif got me."

Ivy nodded at the seven-year-old's oversized blue ring that she'd spied in many quarter machines. "Very pretty."

Ivy smiled at her brother-in-law as he sat across from them. She'd spent many hours in prayer for her sister and new brother-in-law. Married less than a year and already they were the legal guardians of Bella and Benny. Mirela had cared for Benny in a daycare since his birth. Had even taken him and Bella to church on Sundays and Wednesdays. Their mother became addicted to drugs, started burglarizing houses, and ended up incarcerated. Mirela and Josif had been home from their honeymoon only a week when they took in the children.

Now Mirela stayed home with the children while Josif continued to run his family's hotel in Gatlinburg. They were only forty-five minutes from Greenfield, but it had been an adjustment for Mirela and the kids, becoming a family of four and moving away from their home.

As if reading her thoughts, Mirela announced, "The adoption should be finalized next week."

"That's wonderful." Ivy nestled Bella under her arm. "I just hate that you won't be in my class next year."

Bella puckered her lower lip. "Me, too." She brightened. "But I did get to meet my teacher. She seems really nice. I drew a picture of her and showed my mom."

Ivy's mother buckled Benny into the high chair then reached over and patted Bella's hand. "I bet she loved it."

Bella nodded. "She did. Said it was the prettiest picture she'd ever seen."

Ivy glanced at her sister. She didn't know how Mirela

had the strength to allow the kids to visit their mother in prison. Ivy would want to claim the kids as hers and keep them away from the woman who'd put them through so much heartache the last year. But Mirela's heart was as big as the state of Tennessee, and she understood firsthand a child's desire to know their birth parents. She'd been overjoyed when Josif's family—friends of Mirela's birth parents from Serbia—had found her.

The waitress arrived and took their orders then Mirela turned to Ivy. "You ready for school?"

Ivy pushed strands of hair behind her ear. She'd spent most of the day finishing bulletin boards, putting names on lockers and desks, and finalizing lesson plans. After a couple of days of professional development this week and home visits over the weekend, school would start the following Tuesday. "Guess I'm ready as I'm going to be." She pulled her list out of her purse. "Got my kiddos' names right here. Gonna start praying over them tonight."

"Anybody you know?"

"Couple of siblings from a few years back, and…" She noticed her mom open and close her right hand. "Mom, do you need some pain reliever? I have some in my purse."

Her mom swatted the air. "Already took some. I'm fine."

But she wasn't fine, and Ivy knew it. She needed to retire. Many of her mother's friends were already retiring. Some continued to work, but they didn't struggle with arthritis and complete strenuous tasks at work as Ivy's mother did. Having spent years on the mission field with Ivy's dad, her mom started a career later than most people. And she loved her job. Ivy knew her mother's heart would break once she had to quit.

Her heart had nearly broken last year over Mirela and Josif's relationship. For months, she'd been less than pleased with Mirela's growing relationship with Josif's family.

An idea formed in Ivy's mind. Maybe she could think of a hobby for her mom. Something dealing with people, especially people who needed help of some kind. Hmm. It couldn't be too strenuous. Just something to let her know she still had a purpose after retirement.

Their meals arrived, and Josif led them in a quick prayer. Mom pulled off pieces of a roll to give to Benny while the group took bites of their steak and chicken dinners. Ivy felt her mother's gaze, and she looked up.

An expression of pleasure and mischief draped her mother's features. "Saw Brent at the hospital today."

Ivy cringed. Brent was a terrific guy. A great friend. But that was it. Her mother simply would not get the hint. Ivy peeked at her sister. Mirela shoveled in a huge bite of mashed potatoes, and Ivy knew she held back a chuckle. Josif's lips were parted into a ridiculous grin as well. Ivy rolled her eyes and looked back at her mother. "That's great, Mom."

"He said you two had dinner together the other night— your last night at the pantry. You didn't tell me."

"There wasn't anything to tell. We grabbed a burger. We're just friends."

Her mother released an exaggerated sigh, and Ivy bit back a growl. Part of her wished she could just like Brent in the way her mother wanted. She didn't want to disappoint her mom. But Brent didn't like her that way either. It was her mother doing all the matchmaking.

"I invited him to dinner on Friday. Six o'clock."

"Mom, I have home visits scheduled for Friday."

"Not during dinner, I presume."

Ivy clamped her lips shut. She should be done with her last visit before six, but her mother shouldn't just assume she'd agree to a family dinner date. She was twenty-six years old. She may have had plans. A real date even. She huffed. Even if everyone at the table knew that wasn't likely.

Ivy hadn't been on a date since college. Not that she minded. She'd been busy with her job, church, and volunteer work. Her life was complete, even if she had felt a niggling of jealousy every once in a while over Mirela and Josif's obvious affection.

Ivy looked at her mother. "You shouldn't make plans like that without asking me."

"You're home every Friday night. Why would this one be any different?"

Her mother's words were like a punch in the gut. *Way to rub in that I'm a complete dating loser.* She glanced at Mirela and Josif. Both contorted their features into one of pained pity.

"We can come, Gramma."

Ivy smiled at Bella. Saved by the child.

Mirela shook her head. "Remember, you and Chloe are going shopping with Mama Sesely for new outfits for school."

"Oh yeah. I forgot."

Ivy groaned. Even the seven-year-old had Friday night plans. She glanced back at her mother. "Fine, but no matchmaking."

Her mother grinned and placed her hand against her chest. "Me? Of course not."

Ivy shoved another bite of meat into her mouth. Maybe she'd get sick and spend the night in her room.

Carter hadn't been this sick in years. The kids weren't even in school yet, and somehow Lauren contracted a stomach bug that she generously passed on to her brothers. He'd spent the entire night cleaning sheets and floors after the boys failed to make it to the bathroom in time. By morning, the bug hit him.

Though he never would have thought he'd say it, he was glad he didn't have any jobs pressing. He wouldn't have made it through the day.

He pressed a cold rag against his forehead and then wiped it along his cheeks. He'd stopped vomiting, but he continued to battle cold sweats. Still he had to press on. It was almost six o'clock, and the kids had to be fed.

Opening the cupboard, his stomach churned at the sight of canned meat and vegetables. He grabbed a package of spaghetti noodles and sauce. It was a quick, easy meal. He'd fix it then go back to the couch.

The buzzer on the dryer sounded. He groaned, as he knew he had to take the clothes out of the dryer, transfer the clothes in the washer to the dryer, and then add the last load of vomit-clad sheets into the washer. He took a sip of lemon-lime soda and a small bite of a saltine cracker. Hopefully, it would help his troubled stomach as he switched laundry around.

He missed Mary. On days like this the ache in his heart and mind was almost too much to bear. If he hadn't forgotten the formula…he'd just been so busy at the jobsite. Business had been booming two years ago. She'd called and she'd texted him to remember Gabe's formula. But he'd forgotten. And she'd left the house in a huff to get it.

He shook his head, pushing the memory as far back as he could.

"Dad, the boys are hungry. I'll help with supper."

He looked at Lauren, remembering days when he'd returned home to her decked out in purple and pink princess outfits and plastic tiaras. He suddenly realized he hadn't seen her play—really play—in a year, and she was only seven.

She needed a mother. Desperately. But what could he do? He didn't want to date. Couldn't afford to date. And he missed Mary. He wanted his wife back.

He blinked then swiped away the sweat beading on his upper lip. He wasn't going to be able to deal with the laundry. The stench would do him in. "Tell you what, Lauren. If you can take the laundry out of the dryer, put the wet clothes in there, and add the dirty ones to the washer, then I'll start supper."

Lauren nodded as she headed toward the laundry room.

"Don't worry about the soap or starting it. I can do that."

"I know how. I'll do it."

Her tone was flat, and guilt lumped heavier upon his head. His seven-year-old knew how to start the laundry? When had that happened?

Plugging his nose, he opened the can of sauce and dumped it in a pan. He added water to a pan and set it on the stovetop to boil. He pulled the garlic bread out of the freezer. His stomach rolled, and Carter flopped into a chair and dipped his head. "Clay, come here, son."

"Yeah, Daddy?"

Carter looked up at his boy. He still wore the last pair of pajamas Carter had put on him after his and his brother's vomiting competition the night before. Carter took in strands of hair stuck together covering his ears. He needed a bath and a haircut. "I need your help."

"'Kay."

"I need you to open the garlic bread and place the pieces in a row on the cookie sheet."

"What's a cookie sheet?"

Carter pointed to the bottom of the stove. Gabe had wandered into the kitchen. The three-year-old opened the drawer beneath the range. Clay pulled out a cupcake pan. "This?"

Carter shook his head. He started to get up but a wave of nausea overwhelmed him, and he sat down and wiped his face with the cold rag. He swallowed. "It's flat, Clay."

Clay pulled it out, and Carter nodded. He'd get up in a moment and preheat the oven. He just needed to sit a second.

"Get out of the way, Clay!"

Carter looked up in time to see Lauren push her brother away from the stove. She grabbed the cookie sheet from Clay's hand and opened the garlic bread.

Clay cried, causing Gabe to start in as well. A volcano of anger erupted from Clay and he screamed and pushed Lauren. She squinted and pointed toward the living room. "Out! Both of you."

Clay ran out of the room screaming with Gabe close at his heels. Carter's head pounded.

"I don't know how to do the temperature, Daddy."

Carter wiped his brow again and exhaled a long breath. He stood and walked to his daughter. With every ounce of energy he could muster, he knelt to her level. "Lauren, you can't treat your brothers that way. I asked for Clay's help."

"He wasn't doing it right."

"Honey, how would you know that? He was doing a perfectly fine job."

She glared at him, her lips pursed together. Her chin quivered, and Carter knew a little girl still lived inside the hardened shell. *God, when did this happen? What can I do to help Lauren be a little girl again?*

Ignoring the cold sweat that swept through his body, he grabbed her hands. "You are going to your room for a time-out. Before you get there, I want you to find your brothers and apologize. I will call you out when dinner is ready."

She crossed her arms in front of her chest. "You need my help."

"You need to be a little girl. Now go." He pointed toward her room.

She held her ground, lasering him with a look of contempt.

"Now, Lauren. Go."

She turned and stomped toward her room. Carter shook his head. Lauren was too young to act like a teenager. Too young to feel responsible for the family.

At times fearing it was going to kill him, somehow Carter made it through the rest of the meager dinner preparations. He called the children back into the kitchen. Their plates already fixed, they sat in their seats, and Carter determined to sit with them. He couldn't eat, but he would pray and stay with his family.

After prayer, Carter swallowed back the nausea swirling in his gut. He tried not to get sick as he watched the children eat. Afterward, he'd talk to Lauren about dolls and dress up. Tell her he wanted her to act like a little girl. Ask her if she had a friend she'd like to have over to play. He knew there were a couple of girls her age at church. With school starting next week, she'd see some of her classmates from last year as well.

He watched as Gabe grabbed a handful of spaghetti and shoved it in his mouth. Carter nodded toward the utensil on the table. "Use your fork, Gabe."

Before his three-year-old could comply, Lauren huffed and grabbed the fork and reached for Gabe's hand. Carter felt worn to his core over her frustrations with her brothers. He took the fork from Lauren, gave her a warning look that she needed to allow her brother to learn to use the utensil then placed it in Gabe's hand instead. Lauren scowled, and Carter shook his head at her. "He can do it himself."

The three-year-old shoved the fork in the noodles and lifted a huge bite to his mouth. Carter's stomach churned, and a wave of nausea washed over him. He couldn't hold it back this time. He raced into the bathroom and hugged the commode.

After several moments, he sat up and grabbed a towel from the holder.

"I will do it. You go play."

He heard Lauren's voice, louder than necessary as she barked out orders to her brothers. He needed to get her, to tell her to stop acting so mean to her brothers, to stop acting like an adult, to go play with toys.

A volcano erupted inside his gut, and he leaned over again. He'd have to tell her later.

Chapter 3

Carter turned off the vacuum cleaner and wrapped up the cord. Pushing it back to the laundry room, he surveyed the house. It wasn't as clean as Mary would have it, but it was good enough for a home visit from Lauren's second grade teacher.

He scratched his head. He wished he could remember the lady's name. She'd sent a card confirming the date more than a week ago, and he'd misplaced the card. Probably threw the thing away. He wanted to be able to call the woman by her name, but for the life of him, he couldn't remember what that reminder had said.

He shrugged as he shoved the vacuum cleaner in the laundry room and shut the door. Nothing he could do about it. He'd just have to ask her name when she got there. He walked back into the living room. Clay was sprawled across the couch watching a children's program. Carter ruffled the boy's hair, and Clay looked up at him. "You wanna watch my show with me?"

"Wish I could, buddy, but I gotta get ready for Lauren's teacher."

"Is my teacher coming, too?"

Carter smiled. "Not today."

Clay was excited to start kindergarten. Carter prayed the socialization and lessons would encourage the boy. Two years without a mother had been hard on Clay. Difficult for all of them.

Carter made his way down the hall and checked on Gabe. His youngest lay peacefully in his bed, thumb shoved firmly in his mouth. The pediatrician told him it was time to wean Gabe from thumb sucking, but the habit was such a comfort to his son. And Carter simply couldn't snatch that comfort away from him.

Hearing voices coming from Lauren's room, he sneaked a peek inside. She sat on the floor playing with her dollhouse. His heart leaped in his chest. She was playing. As he watched, he realized the mother had been laid to the side. Only the dad and the kids were inside the house. His heart broke at his daughter's reality.

God, I never thought this would be my life. Mary and I wanted so much more for our children.

With a heavy heart, he made his way back down the hall and out the front door to check the mail. He pulled the envelopes out and shuffled through them as he walked back toward the house. He stopped when he read the return address of one of his past clients. His heartbeat quickened as he tore open the envelope. Pulling out a check for the full payment of a job, Carter threw back his head and howled. "Thank You, Jesus."

He'd pay the utility bills and still have enough to get the

kids' hair cut and buy school supplies and a new outfit for Clay and Lauren on their first day. He'd also get groceries to replenish what had been given to him from the pantry. He'd just have to find where he put the list he'd made of what they'd given him.

He glanced at his watch. Three hours until the teacher was supposed to show up. Plenty of time to go to the grocery store. He patted Clay's head. "Get your shoes on, son."

"Where we going?"

He turned at Lauren's voice. He waved the envelope. "Daddy got paid, sweetie. We're going to the store."

Lauren's face brightened, and she raced back toward her room. To get her shoes as well, he assumed. The flashing red light of his answering machine caught his eye. Surely he hadn't missed a call in the short time it took him to check the mail. He was surprised one of the kids hadn't picked up.

He pushed the button and a deep voice filled the room. "Hello, Mr. Smith. James Lorie gave me your number. Said you do good work."

Carter crossed his arms in front of his chest. At least James was spreading the word about his work. He certainly still hadn't paid him.

"Anyway, I'm needing someone to do some tiling and hardwood floor work for me. Actually, I got a couple houses that I'm flipping, and I'll need to know pretty quick... ."

Carter's heartbeat raced again. Could this be true? Payment and a big job all in one day. *God, You really do work it all out. I'm sorry I've been so frustrated. You always take care of everything.*

"We're ready, Daddy. Just Gabe is still asleep." Lauren stood beside Clay. Carter noticed Clay's shoelaces were tied correctly. Carter knew his daughter had helped, as the boy still struggled perfecting the art.

He lifted his finger. "Just one minute."

Not wanting to waste a moment, Carter called the man and set up a time to meet and look at the property so he could give an estimate of the cost. Once off the phone, he made his way into Gabe's room and lifted his still-sleeping son off the bed. Any other day Carter would have let the boy sleep. But today Carter was too excited. He wanted to drop off the bills and pay back the pantry. Tomorrow evening he'd take the kids for haircuts and new clothes.

Gabe smiled at him through heavy lids, and Carter pressed a kiss to his son's forehead. "We're going bye-bye, son."

Gabe nodded and rested his head on Carter's shoulder, thumb still in his mouth. Carter maneuvered him around and slipped on the child's sandals. Gabe started to wake from his dreamland, and by the time they'd made it to the van, was beckoning for a box of juice. Juiced and ready, the family headed to the grocery store after a quick stop at the bank.

"Daddy, can we have gummies?"

Clay held up a box of the silly-shaped fruity treat. It had been a while since they had been able to splurge. It felt good to nod and watch his boy throw the box in the cart.

He glanced at the list again as they made their way to the checkout. He believed they'd gotten everything. The cashier rang them up and he handed her cash. *God, it feels good not to stress, to just hand over the amount.*

With the kids loaded in the car, an idea struck him. He wanted to celebrate. They needed something fun. God had provided, as He always did, and Carter felt such relief and peace that he'd received pay for his hard work. His hands itched with the thought that in a few days' time, he'd use them once again as a provision for his family. Carter said, "Let's get ice cream."

Squeals sounded from the back. He drove through a fast-food drive-through and ordered. The kids ate their fill as they made their way back to the house. Looking at the clock on the dash, he gasped. Lauren's teacher should be there in fifteen minutes. He'd completely forgotten.

Unbuckling the kids, he hurried them into the house.

"What's the matter, Daddy?"

Lauren licked the ice cream, and Carter noted the circle of vanilla around her mouth. He'd have to clean them up and quick.

"Your teacher's going to be here any minute."

Clay walked into the kitchen, tears filling his eyes. His arms were opened and Carter saw that most of the sundae streamed down Clay's front. "I dropped it."

"Yep, you did."

Carter pulled the shirt off his son, only to smash the dairy product into Clay's hair. Carter sucked in a breath. "Go get a new shirt, Clay."

Carter tossed the soiled shirt into the laundry room and shut the door. He grabbed a rag out of the kitchen drawer and wet it. He touched Gabe's face and the boy screamed. "Daddy, cold!"

Ignoring the boy's protests, he finished wiping his face. The doorbell rang, and Carter tossed the rag to Lauren. "Wipe off your face, honey."

He walked to the front door, praying Clay had put on a new shirt, even though he knew the boy wouldn't have run a comb through the ice cream Mohawk. Maybe putting on the shirt would flatten his hair a bit. A man could hope, anyway.

Carter opened the door and his heart sank to his gut. "You?"

* * *

"Carter Smith?" Ivy swallowed the knot that suddenly formed in her throat. How could she not have known the man from the pantry was one of her parents?

She'd read through the names before she'd left that morning. But one of the other students' last names was Carter. Somehow she must have bypassed Carter Smith.

Heat warmed her cheeks. Why hadn't she checked Lauren's parents' names? She knew why. Lauren was the last visit of the day, and she was running late. Plus she was stressing about dinner with her mom and Brent. She cringed as her hands grew clammy. Why hadn't she looked at the name again?

He was cute. So cute. And the house was gorgeous. He was obviously only hurting from the struggling economy. He had to have done well financially at one time to own this house. Why hadn't she recognized the address? It had seemed familiar, but she'd been on so many home visits. Sometimes the addresses blurred together.

Carter continued to stare at her, and her mind replayed what she'd read of Lauren's history. Lauren Eileen Smith. Seven years old. Birthday: September 24. Reads well above grade level. Very articulate. Not as strong in math but still one of the higher scoring students in the class. Sometimes struggles with peers. Natural leader but can be a bit bossy. Mother died in a car accident two years ago. Her first grade teacher shared that Lauren seemed to long for a female role model.

The boy who'd had to use the restroom at the pantry ran into the living room shirtless with his hair standing straight up.

The youngest one ran into the room without his pants. Lauren chased behind him holding a diaper. "He pooped, and I was trying to clean him for my teacher."

Lauren stopped, her eyes big as apples, having spied Ivy for the first time. "Are you my teacher?"

Ivy found her voice. "I am." She nodded to Carter. "May I come in?"

He seemed to come to his senses and shrugged. She noted the tinge of pink at the base of his neck. "Why not?" He smiled, but she could tell it was forced. "Can't get much worse."

He motioned toward the couch. "Have a seat. I'll get my boys cleaned up."

Ivy sat down and took in the American traditional country decor. Blue and red stars on the curtains. Patriotic-looking stuffed bears. He probably hadn't changed anything since his wife's death.

She sat on a sturdy, dark brown leather couch. Took in the oversized television. Furnishings most of the men she knew would like.

Lauren sat beside her. "We got ice cream today. Daddy got paid."

"That's terrific." So, he was a hard worker as she'd assumed. He just hadn't gotten paid. She'd known several families in the same predicament.

Ivy took in the child's blond hair and brown eyes. Such a unique combination, especially since Carter's hair was so dark. Lauren looked at her with adoration. A complete turnabout from the angry, bitter glances she'd given at the pantry.

Lauren clasped her hands. "I love school. I do good in all my classes."

Ivy nodded. "I read that you do very well. I'm looking forward to having you in class. We're going to learn all sorts of things this year."

Lauren frowned. "You read about me? What did you read?"

"Well, that you're seven years old. Your birthday is September 24th—"

"Did you read about my mom?"

Ivy folded her hands in her lap. What should she tell the child? In her experience, honesty always proved the best policy. She cleared her throat. Unsure if Lauren knew the particulars, she picked her words carefully. "I did. I read that your mother passed away."

Lauren looked at the floor. "It was a car accident." She shook her head. "I can't even remember her." She pinched her lips together and furrowed her brow. "If I try really, really hard, I can sorta remember her taking me to school. She was driving in the front seat. I can see her blond hair, but when she turns around her face is fuzzy."

Ivy's heart broke for the girl. So smart. So articulate. And devastated by something a seven-year-old should never have to experience. *God, show me how to encourage this child. Wrap her up in Your arms.*

Carter walked into the room. She wondered how much of their conversation he'd heard. She couldn't decipher his expression. "I apologize things were so crazy when you got here." He settled into a chair across from her. "So, tell us about your class."

Ivy tried to focus on Lauren as she talked about class expectations and goals, even though politeness required she look at Carter every once in a while. The man was entirely too attractive. Dark eyes. Thick brows. Straight nose. Strong chin. Slight cleft.

She had to purposely avoid looking at his physique. Did the man purchase his clothes too tight on purpose? His muscles bulged, ridiculous and tempting. She couldn't believe the urge she fought to touch his arms.

She blinked away the thought. "So, do you have any questions for me?"

Carter shook his head. "I don't think so. What about you, Lauren?"

The girl grabbed Ivy's hand. "I can't wait to start school next week."

Ivy's heart twisted for the child. She couldn't imagine why the first grade teacher said Lauren could be a handful. She must have not had a connection with the child. Lauren was one of the sweetest kids she'd met.

Carter stood. He seemed in a hurry to get rid of her. She prayed her attraction to him wasn't obvious. The very thought horrified her.

He offered his hand to help her up. Ivy swallowed. She didn't want to touch his hand. She might trip over her own feet if she actually touched the man. Telling her inner cavewoman to get a grip, she lifted her hand. When he touched her, tingles shot through her like a high school girl gleaning attention from the quarterback.

"I do have a favor to ask of you."

Ivy forced his words to process in her mind. "Of course. How may I help?"

He pointed to the grocery bags sitting next to the front door. "I'm reimbursing the pantry. Planned to take these over there tomorrow, but I've got a new job and I'm afraid I won't make it in time."

"You want me to take these to the pantry?"

"If you don't mind."

"Sure. Don't mind at all. I'm having dinner with the director tonight."

"Terrific." Carter grabbed several bags. "Kids, come help."

Before Ivy could pick up some as well, his children scooped up what was left and followed their dad to her car. Ivy clicked the doors unlocked, and they loaded up the backseat. Carter shut the door. "It was nice to meet you. Call me if you ever need anything."

Ivy slipped into her car. Lauren stood beside the door. "I'll see you next week, Ms. Adams."

"I can't wait, Lauren."

Ivy's heart drummed a staccato beat as she made her way to the house. It was after six o'clock. She knew her mother would be livid. But her mind whirled from having met the Smith family again. To think Lauren was in her class. *And I have to see that man all year.*

Her attraction to him was crazy. The guy had three kids. He was a construction guy, working odd jobs until the economy allowed him to get back on his feet. Which meant his income and his hours weren't steady.

She pulled into her driveway, thankful Brent must have been running late as well. Before she shut the door, he pulled up and parked on the road. He stepped out of the car and flashed a smile.

Her mother was right. Brent was the kind of guy she should go for. Nice looking. Stable job. No kids. And most importantly, a devoted Christian. Why didn't he make her heart beat faster and her knees go weak?

"Hey, Ivy." He walked up to her car and looked in the backseat. "Let me help you."

"Actually, they need to go in your car."

He furrowed his brow.

"They're repayment from a man who'd had to use the pantry a week ago." She pulled out the grocery card Carter had given her. "He even put money on here to reimburse for the cold items."

"That's great." Brent opened the back door and grabbed several bags. "So, how'd you run into him?"

"His daughter is one of my students. Small world, huh?"

"Very."

With the bags in his backseat, they walked toward the house. "Did I tell you I got tickets to Tennessee's football game this weekend?"

Ivy shook her head.

"You wanna go?"

She bit her bottom lip. She wasn't a football fan. Not in the slightest. She tried to think of a reason to decline. Something that wasn't a lie but wouldn't hurt his feelings either.

"Of course she'll go."

Ivy jumped and turned at her mother's voice behind her. She glared at her mother. Brent meant for them to go as friends. Her mother wanted more.

"Great."

Brent placed his hand on the small of her back, and Ivy felt a moment of panic. He did think of her as just a friend, right?

Chapter 4

Carter popped off the wooden strip from the bathroom's baseboards. He'd received a call from a church friend for a quick tiling job. It would only take a day to finish the tiling, despite the fact he'd had to bring his two older children with him for the job. He'd come in early the next morning to grout the floor. The job for his friend couldn't have come at a more perfect time. School and the large contract he'd received would start the next day.

A smile formed on his lips when he thought of the hardwood and tiling job he would start the following day. The whole house. And not just one house but five of them. From over the phone, the guy had sounded thrilled when he learned Carter was certified to do just about anything in a house. And the things he wasn't certified to do, he knew plenty of guys who'd work for him who could do those jobs. He'd even been able to hire back two of his guys to help with the flooring.

The money he'd make would be enough to pay the bills and living expenses for the next four months. And it would take the three of them less than a month to complete the job. Carter closed his eyes and offered up a quick prayer. *Thank You, God.*

"Daddy, Lauren won't let me watch my show and it's my turn."

Carter turned to look at Clay. He hated having to bring the kids to work with him. His neighbor babysitter had Gabe, but she wasn't able to take Lauren and Clay. Every teenager from church was busy shopping or enjoying the last day of freedom before school started. If Mary were alive it wouldn't be an issue.

Carter called toward the other room. "Lauren, is it Clay's turn?"

"Daddy, it's my favorite show," she yelled back.

"I understand, but is it Clay's turn?"

Silence sounded from the other room.

Clay bobbed his head. "See, Daddy. She won't say 'cause she knows it's my turn."

"Lauren, answer me," Carter called again.

"Yes." She sniffled after the answer.

"Okay. Give the remote to Clay. You get it again next."

Clay scurried back into the other room. Carter turned back to his work when he heard a crash.

"There. You little brat." Lauren's angry voice rang through the house.

Carter walked into the living room. "What is going on?"

Big tears welled in Clay's eyes. Lauren sat beside him, her arms across her chest. "I gave him the remote."

Carter noted the controller on the floor, its back popped off and the batteries scattered. Frustration welled within him. "Lauren, why is the controller on the floor?"

She shrugged.

"She threw it," Clay said as tears streamed down his cheeks.

Lauren glared at her brother.

"That's it." Carter took Lauren by the arm and marched her into the kitchen. He sat her in a chair then knelt to her level. "You are in time-out. And after time-out, you will not watch any more shows today. You will not treat your brother that way. Do you understand me?"

Lauren crossed her arms in front of her chest again and looked away. No sign of remorse.

"Do you understand me?" Carter repeated himself.

"Yes." Her mouth spoke the word, but her body was still hardened with anger.

Hoping the time-out would soften her, Carter stood, walked back in the living room, and fixed the controller for Clay. He made his way back to the bathroom and started back to work.

Anger with Lauren niggled at him. The owners were gone on vacation. They'd been very kind to allow him to bring the kids to their house. She should treat others' things with more respect. And she should be kind to her brother. Lauren's frustration toward her brothers seemed more intense lately.

Parenting didn't come with experience; it was a learn-as-you-go kind of thing. Since she was his first child, he'd never had a seven-year-old before Lauren. Maybe all of them threw fits when they didn't get their way. Possibly all of them were mean to their brothers. But he didn't like it. And he wouldn't stand for it.

As he laid the first tile, his mind wandered to Lauren's new teacher, Ivy Adams. The woman was adorable and melt-in-your-mouth sweet. Lauren would probably devour her the first day of school. The poor lady wouldn't know what to do.

He thought of her long blond hair. It looked so soft, flowing down her back and over her shoulders. Mary had blond hair, but not like Ivy Adams. Ivy's was lighter than wheat and straight as a level. Mary's had more wave to it. Ivy's eyes were the lightest blue he'd ever seen. Mary's were blue, too, but more like the ocean. Ivy's were like the sky on a clear day. They beckoned serenity.

He shook his head. Comparing Mary and Ivy? He shouldn't even be thinking of Ivy as "Ivy." She was Miss Adams, Lauren's second grade teacher. Yet, when he thought of her it was always Ivy. Her name fit her, willowy and beautiful.

She wasn't married. He'd read through the materials she'd brought the night of the home visit. His cheeks burned when he thought of how many times he'd read her letter introducing herself.

She loved the outdoors, camping, fishing, and hiking. Mary would have wrinkled her nose at the thought of a simple hike. He couldn't fathom what she would have been like trying to bait a hook or pitch a tent.

There he went again, comparing his wife and the teacher. Without thinking, he touched his left ring finger. He wasn't married anymore. Hadn't worn his band in a year. Took a year to take it off, but once he did, he hadn't been able to put it back on, either.

Laying a tile in place, he remembered following Ivy to her car. She wore a light blue shirt and white skirt. He hadn't meant to, but he couldn't help but take in how nicely God had formed her. His senses awakened, and he missed Mary all over again.

So much more than just the mother of his children and the caretaker of his home died that night. Their physical intimacy was gone, and two years was a long time.

With a huff, he made his way to the garage to cut a tile

to fit the corner. He tried to focus on the measurement as he inwardly battled things he couldn't have, but missed so desperately.

The back door opened and Lauren stepped outside. "Can I get up now?"

He sighed. He'd forgotten about Lauren. The poor child had sat in time-out for an hour. Feeling like a complete heel, he nodded. "I'm sorry, Lauren. I forgot to tell you to get up. You can watch a television show since I forgot."

Her expression brightened and she went back inside. Concern niggled at him. Probably it wasn't the best idea to let her watch a show after he'd specifically told her she couldn't. Still, he had forgotten to let her out of time-out.

He placed the tile on the cutter. Parenting was so hard. He never knew if he was being too hard or too lenient. Mary always seemed confident. It just came natural to her.

His stomach growled. He peeked through the back door window and noted it was already an hour past lunch. He needed to hurry up. He couldn't believe the kids hadn't complained about being hungry.

There was just too much to do and not enough time to do it. He exhaled a breath. But at least he had this job. He wouldn't complain. He would keep at it, all of it, and beg God to see him through each day. He'd handled the last two years. He could handle more.

Ivy's smile when she waved good-bye after the home visit skirted through his mind. He forced his thoughts back to the job. He couldn't handle thinking about her.

Whatever you do, do it as if you're working for the Lord. The paraphrase of a verse from Colossians repeated itself through Ivy's mind. Brent had already shut his Bible and was getting ready to start prayer concerns and praises for their small Bible study group.

Ivy hopped out of her seat. "Would anyone like a refill before concerns and praises?"

Several lifted their cups, and Ivy chuckled. "I'll just bring the two-liters in here."

"I'll help you, honey."

Her mom got up and followed Ivy to the kitchen. Not a regular member of the small group, Mom joined them since she didn't have to work and it was Ivy's turn to host the Bible study.

"Brent did a great job, didn't he?"

Ivy nodded, trying to act nonchalant. Brent was a terrific study leader, and she didn't want to take away from his gift. But she didn't want to encourage her mother, either.

Her mother continued, "I've always loved that scripture. It was one of your dad's favorites also. Work with all your heart, not for man, but for the Lord." She paused, and Ivy heard an exaggerated sigh. "He reminds me a lot of your father."

Ivy bit her bottom lip as she washed her hands. It had been six years since her father died. She felt as if she'd had so little time with him. He hadn't gotten to see her or Mirela graduate college. Hadn't walked Mirela down the aisle. Wouldn't walk her down the aisle when her time came. Carter Smith's face filtered through her mind, and she pushed the image away. She considered her mom's words. In a way, Brent was like her dad.She remembered his passion for mission work. He'd spent hours talking with people from Serbia. She couldn't recall a lot of specifics, but she remembered the people gawking at her, touching her hair as if they'd never seen anything like it. And they hadn't. Serbs didn't have long blond, almost white hair.

There was one time when a man with a bunch of kids let her dad come into his dwelling and talk with them.

Ivy couldn't believe how many kids there were. She and Mirela sat on the floor with the other children while her dad told the story about Moses and the Promised Land. The people often responded to the story because they were refugees. They understood the Israelites and being an alien in a foreign land.

Her father spoke with such animation, such passion. She could imagine Brent speaking to a group of children the same way. His face shone with awe when he spoke of God's goodness.

But that didn't mean Brent was God's choice for Ivy. Her mom needed to allow things to happen naturally. If Brent was the one, God would show her. She wrinkled her nose. She didn't want Brent to be the one. He was a friend, but she wanted to feel more about "the one."

She wanted her knees to go weak and her toes to curl at his sight. It seemed silly, even to her thinking, but she wanted fairy-tale feelings. She wanted Prince Charming to sweep her off her feet. For a kiss to wake her from her sleep. To be protected from the dragons of the world.

She wanted more than friendship. She wanted happily ever after.

She picked up the two-liters of regular and diet. "Brent is definitely a wonderful guy."

Her mother grabbed the sweet tea from the refrigerator. "Have you decided what you'll wear to the game? I like your UT sweatshirt better than your vest, but if the weather continues as it has been, it will be too warm for a sweatshirt."

"Mom, I'm not in the least bit worried about what I'm going to wear. I hate football. I spent years going with Mirela because she begged me. I was thrilled when Josif came along to take her to games. I can't believe you told him I'd go."

"Honey, it's important to take an interest in what your man likes."

"He's not my man."

"He will be."

Her mother winked and walked out of the kitchen. Ivy looked at the ceiling. *God, I don't know what to do with her. Make her stop.*

She walked back into the living room. Her mother already sat beside Brent. Ivy felt her mother's gaze as she refilled her friends' cups. She turned to glare at her mother when she realized it was Brent staring at her.

Her hands shook as she set the two-liters on a table. He wasn't looking at her as he had even a week before. It was different, and not in a way she liked.

She sat and looked down at her hands. She picked at a piece of skin beside her thumbnail. When she thought of Prince Charming, she didn't think of Brent. She thought of Carter.

She twitched. Where had that thought come from? She didn't think of Carter. It must be his dark hair and strong physique that had her confused. He should make her think of three hurting children—adorable though they were. Unsteady income—although obviously hardworking.

"I have a praise."

Ivy focused on Cheryl beside her. She'd been so wrapped up in her thoughts she hadn't realized they'd started concerns and praises.

"My parents agreed to come to church with me this Sunday."

Ivy smiled and wrapped her arm around Cheryl in a side hug. She was so proud of her. Cheryl had been a constant nemesis to Ivy's sister, Mirela, when they both worked at a daycare. Then Cheryl hit rock bottom and found the Lord.

Since then, her growth in the Lord had soared, amazing to watch.

Ivy's friend from the elementary school held up a piece of paper. "I've got my list to pray over."

Ivy grinned at Angie as she lifted her own list off the floor. "Got mine, too."

Angie went on. "We need to pray over the kids and the start of a new school year tomorrow."

Brent winked at Ivy, and she squirmed in her chair. "Definitely on my list."

"I know I'm just a guest today, but pray for my arthritis. It's been acting up a lot."

Ivy looked at her mother. The woman never mentioned her health. Never. She threw a fit over Mirela falling in love with Josif. She had definite opinions about Ivy's love life, but she never talked about her own aches and pains.

She needed to go to physical therapy. Her mother had refused multiple times, saying her own exercises and warm soaks did the trick. But they obviously didn't.

Mom looked away from Ivy's scrutiny, which sent Ivy's emotions into more of a tailspin. *God, how bad is it?*

She looked at her mother's hands. She'd been flexing and stretching them for as long as Ivy could remember. Brent put his arm around her mother's shoulder and squeezed. "We'll pray for you, Mrs. Adams."

Her mother looked up at him as if he were God's greatest creation. Too bad her mom wasn't twenty-five years younger. Ivy would have set them up.

A smile split Ivy's lips. Maybe that's what her mother needed—a boyfriend. It had been years since their daddy passed away. Mom struggled with arthritis, but aside from that she was still a fairly young, active woman. Fifty wasn't that old.

Ivy bit back a chuckle. Her mother would clobber her if she could read her thoughts. But maybe it was a good idea.

She mentally tallied the single older men in the church. Mr. Bartley was sweet but way too old. He could be her mother's grandfather. Mr. Leeth was a nice guy but a bit too preoccupied with his job. Didn't even make it to church half the time. Mr. Mamry was a nice man. A lot of grand-kids. Nine, if she remembered right.

Ivy lifted her eyebrows. Her mother loved children. Her arthritis even seemed to magically disappear when Mirela brought Bella and Benny to the house.

"If that's all, then let's pray," Brent said. "If you feel led to say anything, then go ahead, and I'll close us."

Ivy bowed her head and closed her eyes. Cheryl started. She praised God for His provisions and prayed for her par-ents. She finished and Angie started. Ivy tried to focus on their words. Tried to allow their prayers to be hers as well. But she couldn't stop thinking about Mr. Mamry.

What did she know about him? His wife passed away several years ago. Even before their family started going to the church. In fact, it seemed like his last two kids were school-aged when his wife died.

She didn't know exactly how old he was. Probably a few years older than her mom. But he still worked. What was it he did? Ivy bit her bottom lip. He was in the medical field.

God, is he a physical therapist? Ivy rolled the question through her mind. She thought he might be. Excitement swelled in her gut. She didn't have to worry about finding her mom a hobby. Didn't even have to worry about finding her a man. She already had one picked out. And he'd been right under their noses for years. She should have thought of the idea eons ago.

Chapter 5

Ivy breathed a sigh of relief when the second dismissal bell rang for the day. She clapped her hands together. "Okay, everyone. I'll walk to the front with you this week. Starting next week, you'll be able to simply leave the room and head straight to the front drive."

Her smallest student, Roger, whom she quickly learned had quite an inquisitive nature, raised his hand. "You mean you won't walk outside with us every day?"

Ivy shook her head. "Nope. You're in second grade now. Only the kindergarten and first grade students have to walk to the front with their teachers."

"But what about cars? We might get runned over," added Roger.

"Run over," Ivy corrected. "And don't worry. That won't happen. Principal Cooper and the music teacher, Mrs. Drury, as well as several other teachers, will stay with you out front until everyone's parents or guardians come to get them."

"But?"

Ivy motioned for the five remaining students—the students who'd already gone had been bus riders—to follow her to the front. She pointed down the far hall. "See, last year your room was in that hall." She turned and waved her hand the distance of their hall. "Now that you're on this side, you have a bit more freedom. After all, you're seven years old."

Lauren puffed out her chest. "Yeah, dummy Roger, we're older now."

Ivy shook her head. "Lauren, we don't talk that way to our friends. I want you to apologize to Roger."

Lauren stuck out her lip and wrinkled her nose, but she apologized. The child had been an angel the entire day, and the quick transformation surprised Ivy.

Ivy walked a few more steps and stopped beside Mrs. Warren, the art teacher. "Mrs. Warren stands right here to be sure everyone makes it safely to the front."

Mrs. Warren waved. "Did everyone have a good day?"

The children nodded, their expressions excited about all they'd done their first day. Ivy loved the start of school. Eyes full of wonder for all they'd learn. Ears ready to listen. In a week's time, all that would change, and the kids would begin to act like kids—making messes, fussing, tattling, needing reminders for rules and expectations. But the first week was almost always easy and fun.

Ivy guided the students past Mrs. Warren. She looked at the clock on the wall. They were a little late, which was to be expected. The buses had to adjust to their routes, and all the students had to learn new dismissal routines.

They walked outside. Cars, vans, and trucks were lined up in three rows in the front driveway. Students raised their hands to notify the teacher when their pick-up vehicle was parked in the boxed-in area directly in front of the school's doors. A teacher would then hold the student's hand and walk them to the car. It was orderly chaos, but perfectly safe.

Roger raised his hand, and Ivy guided him to his truck. He hugged her leg, and she patted his back while she opened the passenger door with her free hand. Smiling at his mother, she helped him inside. "I think we had a good first day."

"Great." His mom, an oversized, middle-aged woman, chortled. "Kid's been yapping about getting back to school for half the summer."

"Wonderful." Ivy shut the door and waved. She could tell Roger had shifted in his seat. Without a doubt, he would fill in his mother about everything that happened that day. He was going to be a lot of fun to have in class.

Within minutes, four of her five car riders had been picked up by their parents. Only Lauren remained. And Ivy worried about that one. Lauren's transportation sheet read that she would ride the bus to her babysitter's most days, but that occasionally her dad would pick her up.

Because riding the bus was the primary directive, she'd told Lauren to get in line with the bus riders. Lauren, however, had been adamant that her dad was picking her up. That he always picked her up on the first day of school. Of course, *always* only meant kindergarten and first grade. Her daddy could have meant for her to ride the bus today.

She inwardly berated herself as the last few students were picked up over the next ten minutes. Principal Cooper walked toward them. She looked at her watch then at Ivy. "It's thirty minutes past pick-up time. Are you sure she was a car rider?"

Lauren stomped her foot. "Daddy said he would pick me up."

Principal Cooper knelt down to her level. "I'm sure he did, sweetheart. He's probably stuck in traffic."

Ivy bit back a laugh at her boss's excuse. Greenfield wasn't a big enough town for someone to get stuck in traffic. Unless it was the car rider traffic at the elementary school at the end of the day. And that traffic had thinned to nonexistent.

Principal Cooper offered Lauren her hand, but the child flinched away and grabbed Ivy's instead. Ivy forced a smile. She knew her boss would want to know why she listened to Lauren about her dad picking her up when her primary transportation was the bus. Ivy's stomach turned. She should have done what she would have for any other student. Followed what the paper said.

"Don't worry, Principal Cooper. I'll take her to my room, and we'll call her father. I know you have plenty of work to do. Lauren can help me get ready for school tomorrow while we find out what's keeping her dad."

Her boss nodded. "Very well." She looked down at Lauren. "I hope you had a good first day."

By the time they'd made it back to the classroom, Ivy's head was spinning. She handed Lauren a couple of cleaning wipes and asked her to wipe off the desks while she looked up her dad's number on the computer.

She tried the number three times from her classroom phone, but each time it went straight to voice mail. Growing more anxious, she called the only emergency contact number in the system. It was a discontinued number.

She closed her eyes and rested her head on the desk. She was going to be in so much trouble. Why hadn't she just put the child on the bus? She could have checked with the brother's teacher to see if he was riding the bus. She rolled her eyes. *Wish I'd thought of that before now.*

"He's not answering?" asked Lauren. She seemed a bit surprised, which only set Ivy to worrying more. She hoped nothing had happened to him. No emergencies.

Determined not to alarm the child, Ivy lifted her head and straightened her back. "No. But it will be fine. You can just keep helping me get everything ready."

"He always picks me up."

"Did he tell you this morning that he would pick you up today?"

"No. But he always does."

Ivy closed her eyes and sighed. When she opened them, she spied her principal standing in the door frame, her arms crossed in front of her chest. Ivy shook her head. "I'm sorry. Of course I'll stay until we get in touch with him."

Her boss pursed her lips. "This is why we follow procedures, Miss Adams."

She walked back down the hall, and Ivy released a groan.

"Are you in trouble?"

Ivy smiled down at Lauren. The concerned expression etched on her features softened Ivy's heart. "No. It's fine. I'm going to try your dad again."

Again, straight to voice mail. By this time, she'd left four messages. All she could do was wait. She opened her filing cabinet. "You want a snack?"

Lauren lifted her eyebrows as she nodded. Ivy pulled out cheese crackers and a couple of plastic cups. She filled the cup and handed it to Lauren. Then she poured some crackers for herself as well. Within minutes, all the preparations for the following day were ready. Truth be told, she was completely ready for every day for the first two weeks of school. She should have been able to go home earlier than normal today.

She glanced up at the clock. School let out a full hour ago. When Lauren's dad learned she hadn't gotten off the bus, he would probably be worried sick. And it was all Ivy's fault.

Carter threw the gear into Park and jumped out. Lauren had to be here. She had to. His neighbor, Anna, called and said Lauren hadn't gotten off the bus. He'd tried to call the school but kept getting a recording. The bus garage wouldn't answer. He had four messages from an unknown number, but for some reason his voice mail would not open. Stupid phone. As soon as he picked up Lauren, he was heading to the store to pick up an upgrade. He was a couple years past due anyway.

Please, God, let her be here.

He raced through the door and into the office. The secretary was gone. Everyone seemed to be gone. It was only 4:30. Shouldn't somebody still be at school? He knocked on the wooden desk. "Anyone here?"

The principal—he'd forgotten the woman's name, although he'd met her last year—walked out from a back office. "May I help you, sir?"

"My daughter didn't get off the bus. Lauren Smith. Second grade."

The woman smiled, and instant relief swelled within him. She was here. He could just feel it. "In Miss Adams's class?"

Carter released a long breath. His heartbeat slowed as relief washed over him. "Yes."

She motioned for him to follow her. "Right this way."

Her cell phone rang, and she pulled it from her pants

pocket. She looked at the screen. "I apologize. I have to take this call."

There was no way he was going to wait for her to finish her phone call. He pointed down the hall. "Down that way?"

She nodded, but stood still as she talked. He could hear voices a few rooms down. He glanced up at the ceiling. *Thank You, Lord.*

"Daddy's just too busy."

He slowed his pace when he heard Lauren's voice.

"He has to work hard to take care of all three of you." This from Ivy.

"I know, but I want to do cheerleading like Rachel." Shuffling of chairs sounded from the room. Ivy laughed, and he wondered what Lauren was doing.

"You'd be a terrific cheerleader. Why don't you ask your dad to sign you up?"

Cheerleading? Of all the things Lauren wanted to do. He could handle soccer or basketball. Even imagined girls liked to do ballet and whatever other dance classes were out there. But cheerleading? Did they even have cheerleading for seven-year-olds?

"Like I said. He's too busy. Sometimes we don't have any money. Daddy works all the time, but some people don't pay him like they're supposed to."

"I'm sorry to hear that."

Carter was sorry as well. Sorry that his daughter knew such things, that she worried about money. He'd grown up in a middle-class family. Never once did he worry about his parents having funds for his many football and baseball camps, equipment, and outings. He hadn't worried about money until he'd started tech school.

He couldn't listen to any more. He clapped his hands as he walked into the room. Lauren and Ivy jumped up out of their seats. Lauren ran to him, and he wrapped her in a bear hug. He lifted her off her feet and held her close. He didn't care that she was too big to be held this way. He'd never been so happy to see her. "Little lady, you had Anna and me worried to death. You were supposed to ride the bus."

Ivy walked toward them. "I apologize, Mr. Smith. I knew the bus was her primary transportation…"

"Don't be mad at Miss Adams, Daddy," Lauren interrupted. "I told her you were picking me up."

"Honey, you knew I had to work today." He looked back at Ivy. She seemed embarrassed as she shuffled her feet. Still, she should have followed his directions. "Besides, I put on your paper that you were riding the bus."

"Don't be mad at Miss Adams." Lauren cupped his cheeks in her hands. "Mrs. Cooper is already mad at her."

A slight gasp came from Ivy's direction, and he looked at the teacher. Crimson dotted her cheeks, making her even more adorable than she already was. His anger subsided and he put Lauren down. "I'm just glad you're all right."

Ivy seemed to study him. Her light blue eyes glistened, and he realized tears welled in them. Their gazes locked, and embarrassment swelled within him. He pushed it away. What was wrong with him? He wasn't in high school. He nodded at Ivy. "Thanks for staying with her."

"Of course I'd stay." She blinked and turned toward her desk. She picked up a sheet of paper. "These are the numbers we have in the system for you. The emergency contact number was disconnected, and I couldn't get through on your cell. Will you check them?"

He looked at the paper. "Well, the last number for my neighbor is a three instead of a two, and I was out of range. Wasn't getting any calls."

She fixed the number then twisted her mouth to chew the inside of her lip. "I hope you won't feel I'm imposing, but I wonder if you'd consider including me on your emergency contact list."

Carter frowned. She seemed like a nice lady and she was cute as she could be, but that didn't constitute him being willing to trust her with his child outside of school hours. "Why?"

"Just so that I could take her home if this ever happened again."

"This won't happen if she rides the bus."

Red tinged her cheeks again. He could tell she felt bad for not putting Lauren on the bus. And he knew his daughter. Lauren had probably been quite adamant that he was going to pick her up.

Ivy seemed to gather herself as she straightened her shoulders. He liked that about her. That she would rally back her confidence.

She nodded. "That's true. However, most students have two or three emergency contact numbers. It's a good precautionary measure, and I thought I would offer."

"Well, thanks for the offer. I'll—I'll think about it."

"Here's my number." She handed him a piece of paper, and he noticed her cheeks reddened. It had been quite a few years since a beautiful woman offered her phone number. "In case you need to get in contact with me."

He grabbed Lauren's hand in his. She wasn't flirting with him. Giving her number had nothing to do with anything except his daughter, and he needed to be sure he kept his thoughts focused. "We'd better head out."

"Daddy, I'm hungry," said Lauren as they headed toward the door. If he had a dime, even a penny, for every time those words slipped from his kids' lips. Did they all have bottomless stomachs?

"Bye, Miss Adams," Lauren called over her shoulder.

"See you tomorrow, Lauren."

They passed Mrs. Cooper in the hall, and Carter remembered what Lauren said about her being upset with Ivy. He stopped the principal. "It was awful nice of her teacher to stay with her. A contact number wasn't correct, and Lauren's instructions for today were a bit jumbled between Lauren and me."

The principal thanked him for his patience, and he and Lauren headed to the van. With seat belts buckled, he started the engine. He looked in the rearview mirror and sighed. He was covered in wood shavings from the carpentry he hadn't expected to do. The slivers framed his nose and were splattered through his hair. Streaks of dirt raced down his forehead and cheeks where he'd sweated through his labor. Glancing down at his clothes, he realized they were equally covered in wood splinters and dirt.

He'd probably left a mess in Ivy's room just from standing in there. It bothered him that she'd seen him in such a mess. He pushed back the feelings. He didn't care what she thought.

"Were you trying to get Miss Adams out of trouble?"

He turned and looked at Lauren in the backseat. "What?"

"When you told Mrs. Cooper she was nice to stay with me?"

Carter turned back around and grinned. "No reason to get your teacher in trouble for something you did."

He looked in the rearview mirror and noted Lauren's face tinged pink. It warmed his heart to know the child knew she'd been in the wrong. Lately, he'd been keeping mental tallies anytime Lauren exhibited remorseful behavior. It hadn't been often enough when it came to how she treated her brothers.

"I really like Miss Adams, Daddy."

"Me, too."

He swallowed when the words slipped through his lips. He feared he liked her a bit too much.

Chapter 6

Ivy wanted to be anywhere but here. She knew her family and friends thought she was weird. But football stadiums grossed her out. Probably thousands of people had sat in her seat. Even now, thousands of people sat around her. She thought of how many people had used the restrooms and shivered. The people who cleaned them most likely didn't take the care she felt necessary.

And she was here for what purpose? To watch a bunch of grown men in spandex pants and plastic pads knock each other down to chase after a piece of leather. She knew most, if not all, of the fans would ban her from the state if they knew her feelings about the game, but the truth was she simply didn't like football. Didn't understand it, either.

The fans cheered at something Tennessee's quarterback had done, and she was pretty sure the guy two seats behind her had just spit a popcorn kernel in her hair. She peeked back at the thirtysomething guy, his face painted orange to match his T-shirt. He held a drink in one hand and a popcorn and hot dog in the other.

Trying to be inconspicuous, she reached up and raked her fingers through her hair. She shuddered. Sure enough. She found a popcorn kernel. She grabbed hand sanitizer from her purse and squirted a glob in her palm.

"Awesome play!" Brent pumped his fist. "Did you see it?"

Ivy nodded. She didn't know how to respond. She'd seen it. Didn't know what it was called, though she guessed she did know it was good, since the guy made the touchdown. She knew that much, at least. The purpose was to get the pigskin past the opposing players and the last white line.

She pulled out a stick of gum from her purse, unwrapped it, and folded it into her mouth. She offered a piece to Brent. He shook his head. "You sure you don't want something to eat?"

"No thanks." She patted her stomach. "I'm saving my appetite for dinner."

Brent smiled, and his eyes twinkled with a look she didn't want to see from a friend. He was beginning to like her. All her mother's matchmaking was starting to pay off. Only one problem. Ivy's feelings hadn't changed.

Ivy looked at the scoreboard. Only four minutes left in the game. Four minutes could drag on forever. Regardless, she'd focus on the men in tights and not on Brent. She'd select the most unromantic restaurant she could think of for dinner. And when he took her home, she'd reaffirm their friendship, hop out of the car, and not allow her mother anywhere near Brent.

The game ended with Tennessee winning by two touchdowns. Ivy sucked in a breath when they stood to exit the stadium. She hated crowds. Getting out of the congested place made her feel claustrophobic. Brent kept his hand in the small of her back as they weeded their way out of Neyland Stadium. Finally at the car, Ivy exhaled a sigh of relief as she slipped inside.

She squirted a dollop of hand sanitizer in her hand and Brent laughed. She speared him with a glare, knowing he was about to tease her. "You know what they say, cleanliness is next to godliness."

Brent laughed. "Ivy Adams, you know that's not true."

Ivy elbowed him as she laughed. "It works for me."

"Don't worry, I love your quirks. Where we gonna eat?"

The tone in his voice caused Ivy to pause. She had to make sure he knew they were just friends. "How 'bout the new hamburger place that opened last month?"

"Great place. Have you eaten there?"

She shook her head.

"Their hamburgers are delicious. The best I've ever eaten." He peeked at her as he took a left turn. "You don't mind that our first date is to a burger joint?"

"Why would I mind? We're just friends."

Ivy kept her gaze focused on the road, even though she knew he studied her a bit longer than he should have for a person who was in the act of driving a vehicle.

He pulled into a parking space and shifted toward her. "Ivy, I…"

Ivy opened the car door. She looked at him and flashed her brightest smile. She did not want to discuss whatever it was she feared he was thinking. "Come on. I'm starving."

The line was too long; the place too crowded. But she didn't want to venture anywhere else. She hated feeling squished with strangers, but she didn't want to go somewhere more intimate with Brent.

She ordered her burger and fries then her cell phone started ringing. While Brent paid, she stepped outside the restaurant so she could answer. She looked at the number on the screen. It looked familiar but she wasn't sure whose it was. She pushed the Talk button. "Hello."

"Hi, Miss Adams. It's Lauren."

Ivy flinched at the sound of Lauren's voice. How did the child get her cell phone number? Then she remembered she'd given it to Carter the first day of school. She'd hoped he wouldn't think she was trying to hit on him. If she had been, it wouldn't have done any good because this was the first time she'd heard from him, and it wasn't him. It was his daughter.

"Hey, Lauren. How are you doing?"

"I'm good."

Lauren didn't say anything else, and Ivy frowned. There had to be a reason for her call. "Is everything all right?"

"Yep." The girl's voice sounded cheerful. "I finished my haiku."

Ivy grinned. So that was it. She wanted to share her work. Well, Ivy loved to hear the creativity of her students. "You wanna read it to me?"

The sound of papers shuffling filtered through the phone. Then Lauren's voice came back on, clear and strong with exaggerated syllables. "My dad is the best. He loves me and my brothers. But sometimes he is mean."

Ivy bit back a giggle. Sounded a whole lot like many of the haiku she'd read from her students over the years. "That's terrific, Lauren. Except your last line has six syllables instead of five. Clap it out and you'll see what I'm saying. Maybe if you take out the first word."

Lauren clapped each syllable as she read the last stanza aloud again. The child grew quiet, and Ivy envisioned her with her mouth puckered and pushed to one side as she bit the inside of her lip. "I guess that works. So, what are you doing?"

"I'm getting ready to eat a hamburger. What are you doing?"

Brent motioned from inside the restaurant that their food was ready. Ivy nodded and lifted her pointer finger for just one more minute.

"Daddy's getting ready to take us to get some clothes."

"How fun. Does he know you're on the phone?"

As if hearing her words, she heard Carter's voice in the background, asking Lauren who was on the phone.

"It's Miss Adams."

A shuffling sounded and Carter's voice sounded. "Hi. Did you need something?"

Ivy flinched at his irritated tone. "I didn't call. Lauren called me to share her haiku poem."

"I'm sorry. I didn't know she had my phone. Okay. Bye then."

Before he hung up, she heard Lauren whine that she didn't get to say good-bye. Then the phone clicked off. Frustration swelled in Ivy's chest. The man didn't have to be so grumpy. She didn't care that Lauren had called to share her poem.

Her cheeks warmed that he thought she'd called him. What? Did he think she spent entirely too many moments of her day thinking about him and his children? She rolled her eyes. Well, he didn't know she did.

Looking into the restaurant, she spied Brent in the far corner. He hadn't started eating. Probably waiting on her. He was such a nice guy. A low growl murmured from her chest. She just wanted to get this date over with and go home.

Carter pushed the stroller into the department store. He hated shopping as much as he loathed not getting paid. Actually, he hated not getting paid more.

Clay stood beside him as he was supposed to, but Carter had to crane his neck to see Lauren several steps behind. "Come on, Lauren."

"Can I have this, Daddy?"

Carter took in the sparkly, pink, miniature-sized purse and had to force himself not to wrinkle his nose. He had the money right now, and business was picking up. He'd had to hire back two additional workers for some electric work for which he'd been contracted.

Still, he wanted to be a good steward of the resources God provided. He'd spent too many months scrounging money, food, anything he could. He patted her head. "That looks more like a Christmas or a birthday present instead of school clothes."

Lauren puckered, but he held his ground and nudged her to the girls' section of the store. He reached inside Gabe's backpack where he kept a change of clothes for his youngest son. He pulled out three small suckers and gave them to the kids. Anna had given him the idea, and so far, it worked like a charm. They'd made it through purchasing clothes for Clay and Gabe. Lauren was the only one left.

He scanned the girls' section. Not like the boys' area at all. Girls had too many options. Skirts and pants. Shorts and tights. Sweaters that buttoned, that had lace, that had sparkles. And some of the shirts looked entirely too provocative. Even for a seven-year-old.

"How 'bout this, Daddy?"

Lauren held up a pink-and-brown leopard-print getup with a short shirt, pink tights, and a vest with fur on the bottom. It was ridiculous. He pointed at the hanger. "You like that?"

Lauren nodded, and Carter furrowed his brow. The outfit was awful. "Let me see what size you are."

He twisted the neckline at the back of the shirt that was

a bit too small for her. Selecting the size up, he grabbed the atrocious outfit and draped it over the back of the stroller.

Lauren rushed to another rack and picked up a gray shirt with a shiny silver star and a rainbow on the front. Silently, he wished her school had a uniform dress code. His life would be simple. No mall. No pink leopard outfits. No shimmering stars.

"Is there anything I can help y'all with?"

Carter looked at the young sales associate with short, choppy brown hair. The girl couldn't have been over twenty. Cute, but wore a bit too much makeup, and since when did girls wear feathers for earrings? However, she looked like the kind of girl who would know just how to help Lauren.

"Yes." He pointed to his daughter, whose expression belayed she wasn't sure if she wanted the woman's help. "I need to purchase about five outfits for her."

The sales associate smiled. "Girls a little tougher than boys to buy for?"

Carter laughed. "Absolutely."

"Why don't you and your boys have a seat right there, and I'll help your daughter?" The lady pointed to a fake-leather purple couch beside the dressing rooms. Carter noted the black fingernail polish and skull-and-crossbones painted in white on her thumbs. He wrinkled his nose. If he didn't feel at a complete loss and utterly exhausted, he would help Lauren himself. She knelt in front of Lauren. "I'm Madi. What's your name, sweetie?"

Lauren pinched her lips closed.

Carter opened his mouth to reprimand Lauren when the woman pulled the leopard outfit off the back of the stroller. "This will look so cute on you. We have some brown boots that would match it perfectly."

Lauren's face lit up, and to Carter's surprise, she reached

up and grabbed Madi's hand. He pushed the stroller to the couch and plopped down. From this vantage point, he could see Lauren and Madi from anywhere in the store. He exhaled a long breath.

"I'm wore out, Daddy."

Carter ruffled Clay's hair. "Me, too, son. As soon as Lauren gets her clothes, we're heading out of here." *And hopefully, I won't have to come back to the mall until it's time to shop for Christmas.*

"I hungry, Daddy." Gabe tried to squirm out of the stroller.

Carter tapped Gabe's hand rest. "No. You stay there. You just ate a sucker."

Gabe leaned back. "I know, but I hungry."

Carter sighed and shook his head at the biggest bottomless pit in the family. He grabbed the backpack off the stroller and rummaged through it. Finding a package of gummies, he ripped them open. "You have to chew each piece, right?"

Gabe nodded. "I know, Daddy."

He handed his son a gummy. The dark-haired urchin popped it in his mouth and chewed with fervor, swallowed, then opened his hand for another. Carter studied his boy as he placed another in his hand. Gabe was the only child who looked like him. Dark hair. Dark eyes.

He looked at Clay with his light blond hair, just like Mary's. Lauren was more of a mix, her hair a dirty blond color. But both of them had their mother's light blue eyes.

Scanning the store, he spied Madi pulling an outfit off the rack for Lauren to look at. Lauren's eyes lit up and she nodded. She obviously liked the lime-green-and-black striped getup. A twinge of pain laced through him. If Mary were alive, she would be the one helping Lauren. She'd know the latest styles. Get excited with their daughter over the goofy-looking attire.

He missed Mary a lot lately. Pushing away the sadness that threatened to wash anew over him, he pulled his phone out of his pocket to see if he'd missed any calls or texts in their hustle from one store to the next. Spying the call Lauren had made to her teacher that afternoon he leaned back on the couch.

He'd been rude to Ivy when he took the phone from his daughter. Hurt Lauren's feelings, too, when he didn't let her say good-bye. But Ivy haunted him. He didn't know why but the woman would not get out of his mind.

"'Nother, Daddy."

Carter leaned up and put another gummy in Gabe's hand.

"Can I have one, too?" asked Clay.

He pulled the other pack out of the backpack. "You can have your own."

Clay's face lit up as he plopped beside Carter on the couch and fumbled with ripping open the packet. Carter watched his son's determination until he finally got it opened. The boy beamed as he plopped one gummy after another in his mouth.

His first son might look like his mother, but that determination came from his dad. *Which is why I know I will stop thinking about that teacher. I have no business entertaining thoughts about her.*

Lauren waddled toward him, loaded down with several outfits. "I'm trying all these on, Daddy."

Madi pointed toward the registers, and Carter realized a line had formed. "I need to go to the register, but if you need anything else just let me know."

He waved. "Thanks for your help."

He and the boys watched as Lauren tried on one outfit

after another. An hour passed and they finally decided on five outfits. By that time, he was exhausted and the boys were cranky. He wished he knew they would go home to a hot-cooked meal. If Mary were still alive, they would have.

Ivy swept through his mind. He wondered if she could cook. He shoved the thought away as he paid for the clothes. It did not matter if Ivy Adams could cook. "Kids, let's go get a hamburger."

"Out to eat?" Lauren squealed.

He nodded. All three of them cheered, and Carter determined to put all notions of women and cooking out of his mind. He would focus on his kids.

Chapter 7

Ivy clapped her hands in a rhythm to let the students know to stop their work and look at her. "It's almost time to leave. Bus riders, you may go get your things from your locker."

Most of the class hustled out of their seats and into the hall. Ivy headed toward the door to be sure everyone behaved as they should and got all their materials.

"Miss Adams, can you help me with my math?"

Ivy looked down at Roger, who was tugging on the bottom of her sweater. "What are you supposed to do to get my attention, Roger?"

He lowered his gaze and raised his hand. He should have remained in his seat, not practically stand on her toes. She had to bite back a giggle as she asked, "Yes, Roger?"

"Can you help me with my math?"

Ivy motioned for him to go back to his chair. "I can and I will as soon as the bell rings to dismiss the bus riders."

She turned to help another student get her papers in

her backpack when a crash sounded. Ivy jumped and saw Roger on the floor, Lauren standing beside him.

She raced to Roger and helped him up. "What happened?"

Tears welled in his eyes as he pointed at Lauren. "I didn't do nothing. She pushed me."

Lauren lifted her chin and jutted out her jaw. "Did not."

"You did, too," another student tattled.

Lauren glared at the girl, and the child slinked back to her chair. Ivy helped Roger back into his seat then motioned for Lauren to step into the hall. She knelt to her level. "Why did you push Roger?"

Lauren folded her arms across her chest. "I didn't."

"Are you being dishonest, Lauren?"

"What's dishonest?"

"Are you lying?"

Lauren's lower lip quivered, and Ivy knew the child was about to confess. She pointed back toward the classroom. "Roger doesn't need help. He just wants attention. He likes you. I don't want him to."

Ivy blinked back her surprise as Lauren wrapped her arms around Ivy's shoulders. "You're my Miss Adams. Not his."

Ivy furrowed her brows. "I am your teacher, but I am Roger's teacher also. You may not treat your friend that way."

The bell rang to dismiss the bus riders. She couldn't talk anymore with Lauren, as the buses ran a tight schedule. She motioned inside the room for the bus riders to leave then bent down to hug Lauren. "I care very much about you, Lauren, but I will have to call your daddy about this."

Lauren stuck out her bottom lip and nodded.

"Now, have a good weekend." Ivy hugged the girl again then sent her toward the buses.

She'd noticed Lauren being clingier with her as each day passed. Lauren seemed to have reverted to acting younger than her age and struggled getting along with her peers. Ivy sucked in a deep breath as she walked back in the classroom and toward Roger. She dreaded calling Carter Smith. It took her days after an encounter with him to get the man out of her mind.

With the school day over, she drove to the house to pick up her mother. Mom took her time getting out of the house and meandering down the walk. Ivy stuck her head out the car window. "Come on, Mom. You're going to be late."

"I don't want to go to the physical therapist."

"Doctor said it will make your arthritis feel better. So come on."

Her mom harrumphed as she slid into the passenger's seat. She pouted the entire ride over, but Ivy ignored her. Once at the office, Ivy signed her in, and they waited to be called back.

The door opened and Mr. Mamry stepped outside. Ivy acknowledged he was a nice-looking, older gentleman. Salt-and-pepper hair, clean-shaven face, fit physique. He was a terrific match for her mom.

"Come on back, ladies." They followed him down the hall and into another room. "I believe I recognize you girls from church."

Her mother nodded but stayed close-lipped.

Ivy piped up. "Yep. I'm Ivy Adams. This is my mom, Sarah."

"It's a pleasure to meet you. I fear I am not as friendly as I should be at church. Always playing with the little ones."

"How many grandchildren do you have, Mr. Mamry?" asked Ivy.

"Please, call me Phil." He lifted both hands. "I have

nine. They are such blessings." He looked at her mom. "Do you have any grandchildren?"

Her mom's eyes lit up, and she sat straighter. "Well, I will have two through adoption. My other daughter only recently got married, but they are adopting children she's taken care of for over a year."

"That's wonderful. Any sons?"

"No. Just the two girls. How 'bout you?"

Ivy sat back in the chair. Phil and her mother hit it off just as she expected. A full fifteen minutes passed before Phil realized he still hadn't read her doctor's orders. Her mother's face challenged a cherry for color when he asked if she'd allow him to take her to dinner.

Her mother placed her hand against her chest. Ivy watched her swallow hard. "I think I'd like that."

Ivy almost fell out of her chair. The man just officially met her mom, asked her out, and her mom agreed. She thought she'd have months of work ahead of her to get the two interested in each other.

They stood to walk out of the office, and Ivy realized it felt a little weird to have her mother going out on a date. *I guess I hadn't really thought that through. Mom with another guy.*

Her mother patted her leg once they sat back in the car. "Now see how easy that was."

Yeah. It was a little too easy. Queasiness found its way in Ivy's belly.

Her mom continued, "So the next time Brent asks you out, all you have to do is say yes."

"Mom, I don't like Brent like that."

"Well, I don't know if I like Phil like that either. How will I know if I don't try?"

Ivy's stomach rumbled. She was hungry, but it was more than that. "Mom, you haven't dated since Dad's death."

"I know." Her mom clasped her hands in her lap. "And, I started to say no. I've never even considered another man. But something in my gut told me to say yes."

Ivy bit her bottom lip. She wanted her mother to be happy. Ivy was the reason her mother came to physical therapy in the first place. She just hadn't expected the matchmaking to work so fast. *Fifty-plus-year-olds sure don't mess around.*

"Who knows? Maybe God brought us together."

Ivy focused on her driving. She hadn't even considered asking God how best to handle her mother's meddling. She'd been manipulating the situation all on her own. *Forgive me, Lord. You are in complete control of who we meet and when we meet them. Who You have for Mom. Even me.*

Lauren's pouty face as she walked away from Ivy at the end of the day filled her mind. The child needed a mother figure so desperately. Ivy wondered if her frustrations were magnified because the child only had brothers.

God brought that child into her life at this time. Ivy had been given the opportunity to make an impact on that little girl's life. She just had to trust God to show her how to do it.

I've also got to call her dad. Ivy cringed. Was Carter Smith in her life for a reason as well? He sure had a way of taking over her thoughts. She could still feel his bicep beneath her fingertip if she thought about it.

They passed a few restaurants, and Ivy's stomach growled. "Fast food okay?"

"Sounds good to me."

Ivy pulled into one of her favorite chicken places. She and her mother walked inside.

"Miss Adams!"

Ivy looked in the direction of the squeal. Her heart felt

as if it fell into her stomach. Lauren waved and raced to her, wrapping her arms around her waist. "Hi, Lauren."

Carter waved. His smile seemed forced.

"Sit with us, please."

Ivy looked down at the girl. "Well, we..."

"Please, please, please!"

She looked at Carter, and he shrugged.

Ivy sucked in a deep breath. "Okay."

Carter watched Ivy and the woman he assumed to be her mother as they placed their orders. The woman looked back at him several times. He sighed as he picked a waffle fry off the ground. He hoped the older woman liked being around kids. If not, his would probably do her in.

Not wanting to look like the sloppiest parent on the face of the earth, he wiped up the boys' mouths and cleared some of the trash from the table. His hands trembled. Why did Ivy have to wreak such havoc on his senses?

The women approached holding their trays. Lauren moved all the way to the inside of the booth. "You can sit by me."

Thankful they'd chosen a larger booth, Carter sucked in a breath as Ivy and then the other woman slid into the booth across from him.

Ivy pointed to the woman. "This is my mother, Sarah."

"I'm Lauren," his daughter piped up and shoved her hand in Sarah's face.

Sarah shook her hand. "A pleasure to meet you." She looked at Clay. "And you are?"

"Clay," said Carter, then he patted his youngest son's head. "And this is Gabe."

"What a lovely family." She extended her hand to him. "And you are?"

"Carter Smith."

"Well, Carter. Your children are beautiful. Is your wife working?"

Before he could answer, Lauren spoke. "Our mom died two years ago."

Carter watched as Ivy mutilated the napkin in her grasp. They locked gazes, and her neck and cheeks darkened. He wanted to touch her cheek, feel its softness, tell her not to be embarrassed. He cringed.

"I am so sorry," said Sarah.

Carter forced himself to look back at Ivy's mother. "It's okay."

Sarah took a bite of her sandwich while Ivy ate a fry. Gabe reached for Sarah's fries, and the older woman laughed and handed him one that was already on his napkin.

Carter noticed how Lauren paid close attention to Ivy's every move. Even mimicked the way she ate. He knew Lauren loved her teacher, but he hadn't realized how attached she'd become. He wondered if that was normal.

He remembered her wearing Mary's shoes and toting her mother's purses around the house when she was about Gabe's size. A girl needed a mom to look up to. At least, his girl did.

"Do you and your family go to church, Carter?"

Carter blinked and looked at Sarah. "Yes ma'am. We go to New Hope on Main Street."

Sarah nodded. "Wonderful church."

"We go to First Community on Ridge Street," said Ivy. Her voice sounded softer than it had the night of the home visit or that day at the school.

"Daddy, can we go to First Community?" asked Lauren. Carter noticed she had wrapped both her arms around one of Ivy's.

He furrowed his brow. "Honey, let your teacher eat her food."

"But I like my church," whined Clay.

"We're not leaving our church, son." He turned to Lauren. "No, we can't go to First Community."

Lauren stuck out her lower lip and folded her arms in front of her chest in a huff. He fumed at her behavior, knowing they warranted consequences when they got home.

Sarah excused herself to go to the bathroom, and Carter watched as Ivy exhaled a long breath. She seemed nervous. Surely she couldn't tell he was attracted to her. He'd tried not to gawk at her, not to think about her.

Gabe lifted his cup to take a drink and his lid popped off. He screamed as the dark soft drink spilled down his shirt. Ivy responded faster than he. She yanked Gabe out of the high chair and pulled off his shirt. Grabbing napkins from the table, she wiped off his chest. "No worries, Gabe. It's okay."

Carter marveled at how quickly she handled the situation. He righted the cup and mopped at the mess with some napkins. "Thanks, Miss Adams."

She turned toward him. "Surely, you don't think of me as Miss Adams."

His throat clogged, and he shook his head. "I don't."

Again, their gazes locked, and Carter yearned to let himself go, to take flight in those light blue eyes. Then she blinked, breaking the moment. "Do you have a change of clothes? I'll take him to the restroom and clean him up."

He couldn't talk. He grabbed the bag off the seat and handed it to her. She stood, and for the first time he noticed her mother standing behind her. Sarah's expression had shifted. She'd smiled at him earlier. Now she peered at him, as if he were the monster who'd come to claim her child.

He was attracted to Ivy. To deny it would be a bold-faced lie. But he knew better. Her mother had nothing to worry about. What kind of life could he offer Ivy? He still loved his wife. Had three children. Still worried over keeping consistent work.

After cleaning the mess, he wiped Lauren's and Clay's faces. Sarah still hadn't said anything to him. Simply studied him. He wondered how long it would take Ivy to clean up Gabe. His face warmed. He hoped she hadn't had to change his diaper. The boy was well past his time for potty training, but the child simply refused to use the toilet. Carter assumed their confused schedule was partly to blame.

He looked at Sarah. It felt weird not to say something to her. He cleared his throat. "Lauren loves your daughter's class."

"That's good." Sarah responded, but it was obviously only out of politeness.

Lauren tapped the woman's shoulder. "I do. She's my favorite teacher ever."

Sarah smiled—a genuine expression—at his daughter. "Here we go."

Carter stood and turned when he heard Ivy's voice behind him. His heart skipped a beat at the sight of his youngest with his face nestled against her shoulder, his thumb in his mouth and his free hand twirling her hair. The euphoric look on her face did not help his determination to keep her out of his mind.

She shouldn't enjoy cleaning soft drinks off his son. It should have been a frustrating task. Now, he would go to bed thinking and dreaming of that beautiful expression on her face.

"We needed our diaper changed, too." She tried to hand him to Carter, but Gabe held tight to her neck.

The smile that parted her lips drew him. And he realized how desperately he wished to press his lips against hers. She must have seen the warning in his eyes, but instead of backing away, a dreamy look wrapped her gaze.

He looked away from her. This could not be happening. He loved Mary. He would always love Mary.

He motioned for Clay to slide out of the booth and stand beside him. Lauren had already slid out from her side. Without looking at her, he grabbed Gabe from her grasp. "Thanks so much for your help." Turning to her mother, he nodded. "It was a pleasure to meet you."

Lauren gave Ivy one last hug before Carter nudged her toward the door. He didn't look back. Hoping he hadn't come across too rude to the women, he buckled the kids into their booster seats.

Once home, he gave them all baths and read stories before it was time for bed. Tons of laundry awaited him. Dishes were still in the sink. But he needed some unwind time. He flopped into bed and turned on a football game.

Ivy's blue eyes, all content and dreamy, popped into his head. He closed his eyes and begged God to take his feelings for her away. They weren't even feelings. It was purely physical. He didn't really know much about the woman.

But, boy, did he want to get to know her. He wanted to take her for a hike, to dinner, to a movie. She cared about children. She'd handled Lauren's overt attention with a tenderness he would have never had the patience for. His attraction was more than physical. He knew that. But it didn't matter. He would never allow himself to love again.

He couldn't just lie in bed and watch a game. He got up. Might as well do the laundry.

Chapter 8

By eleven, he'd finished three loads of laundry, washed the dishes, and cleaned the bathrooms. He was too tired to think about teachers with long blond hair. After changing out of his clothes, he flopped into bed.

It had been raining since they got home from the restaurant. Heavy rain. Curious about the weather forecast, he turned on the news. His chest tightened as he listened to the meteorologist warn of flash floods in their area.

Despite the physical exhaustion, his mind replayed the night his wife died. *"Don't forget Gabe's formula. We're completely out."* Mary's voice still haunted him.

He'd been so busy that week. Business was booming. He hadn't been able to hire enough men to do all the work he'd been contracted to complete. He left home before the sun rose and didn't return until it had gone to bed hours before.

He'd forgotten the formula.

"Carter, I told you we were out. Completely. Not even a bottle left. If Gabe wakes up in the night..."

He tried to apologize, but she shot him a look of death. *"Apologies wouldn't do any good,"* she'd fussed, as she'd tied her shoelaces. *"I'll just have to go myself."*

She'd grabbed her raincoat out of the closet. He should have gone. He knew it. The rain was pouring in what seemed like one bucketful after another, but he was so tired. Barely keeping his eyes open through the shower, he'd fallen into bed once he finished.

Returning to present day, he clicked off the television, rolled to his side, and smashed a pillow against his chest. He'd received the phone call an hour later. Mary had crossed the bridge. The one he'd told her many times not to cross when the rains were heavy. It was a shortcut to the store. Her car had been swept away, and she drowned.

He scrunched his eyes shut, begging God to take the memories away. If he'd only just remembered that formula. She'd still be here. He'd be nestling her, not a cold, hard pillow.

"Daddy, I'm scared."

Carter opened his eyes and saw Clay standing in his doorway. Normally, he'd take the children back to their beds and tuck them in again. But he wondered if the rain haunted Clay as it did him.

He patted the bed. "Come on. You can sleep with me."

Clay's face lit up. "Really?"

"Just tonight."

"Me, too," Lauren sounded behind him.

He shouldn't have been surprised. Lauren was the lightest sleeper. If the rain hadn't awakened her, Clay's footsteps to his room would have.

"You, too."

Clay hopped in the middle, and Lauren cuddled in beside her brother. The two wiggled and argued until Carter said, "Enough. Settle in or back to your beds."

The twosome settled down, and Carter rolled to his back. The rain continued its beating against the roof. He stared at the ceiling, his eyes already adjusted to the darkened room. He would never be able to forgive himself.

"You've been forgiven every sin you've ever committed. You must forgive yourself of this."

He scrunched his eyes shut again. *God, I want to. I want to be rid of this pain. This guilt. But I took their mother. My wife.*

"Your ways are not My ways. I know the beginning and the end. I have a plan for you and your children."

Carter rolled to his side. He and the Spirit had had this conversation more times than he could count. For a moment, Carter would lay his guilt at the foot of the cross. Then Lauren would lash out at her brothers or Gabe would ask if a complete stranger looked like his mommy, and Carter would take it back.

The guilt weighed him, like a bulldozer sitting on his back. He wanted to be free. Wanted it so bad. His eyelids grew heavy.

When he opened them again, it was daylight. The sun wasn't shining, the rain continued to pound, but it was morning just the same. He looked at his clock. If he didn't hurry, he'd be late for the job.

Hopping out of bed, he looked at Lauren and Clay. They were cuddled together, and Carter's heart warmed at their affection. Even if it wasn't conscious. He got ready quickly then made some coffee. By the time the brew had finished, Anna's teenage daughter knocked at the door.

Carter opened it wide and smiled at the thirteen-year-old. "You ready to make some money?"

She shut her umbrella, shook off the excess water, then leaned it against the door frame. "Duh!"

Carter elbowed Jocelyn in the shoulder. The girl had been no taller than his kneecaps when he and Mary built this house. Now she was big enough to babysit his three kids.

"Okay. You know the rules."

She rolled her eyes. "No boys. Like my mom would let me have a boyfriend, anyway. Don't stay on the phone or Facebook." She spread her arms open. "Dude, we go through this every time, and every time you come home to a clean house and happy kids."

She grinned, and he noted the twinkle in her eye. He gently punched her shoulder. "Be good, Jocelyn."

"As always. The kids eat yet?"

He grabbed his raincoat out of the closet. "Nope. Still sleeping."

"Got it." She saluted him as she grabbed the door handle. "Enjoy your day, Smith."

He frowned up at the sky. "Looks like it's going to be a good one."

Jocelyn laughed as she shut the door behind him. He heard the lock latch, and he ran off the porch and into the van.

Today would be anything but enjoyable. He hoped people would stay indoors unless it was absolutely necessary to go out. He thought of the bridge where Mary's car had been swept away. Offering up a quick prayer that no one would try to cross it, he started the van.

He thought of Ivy. It was Saturday. She shouldn't have any reason to *have* to go out. He touched his cell phone in his front pocket, fighting the urge to call her and warn her about the roads. He couldn't. *God, please have her stay home today.*

* * *

"I sure wish I could have stayed home today," Ivy said out loud to herself as she drove toward the pantry. The ground was saturated, ditches filled with water, creeks flooded. She dreaded going past the middle school. The drainage was exceptionally bad, and the road often flooded during heavy rains.

Her cell phone rang, and she picked it up off the passenger's seat and answered it.

"I don't want you to try to go to the pantry today." She recognized Brent's voice. "I'm not going in myself."

"Welp, too late for that." Aggravation niggled. He should have called an hour ago. He knew she left early. "I'm already on my way."

"You're talking to me while you're driving?" Brent's voice raised an octave.

"No worries. I'm driving at a snail's pace, and nobody's on the road with me."

"Guess I'm going in. I'll see you in a few minutes. Ivy, be careful."

The sincere worry in his tone added an extra dose of guilt to her already guilty conscience. Her mom asked her not to try to venture out, stating that the meteorologist said to stay indoors. But she had been determined. She didn't want Brent to have to stock the pantry by himself.

Now, he was going to try to tackle this monsoon—all because of her. She smacked the top of her steering wheel. She should have called him before she left.

She couldn't change things now. Focusing her sights on the road in front of her, she looked past the window wipers and beating rain.

The middle school was just ahead, and it appeared the road was flooded as she feared. Pretty deep, too. The only other way to get to the pantry would be to turn around, drive all the way across town, and then back around toward the middle school. The pantry was only a few blocks down from the school.

She straightened her shoulders. "I'm sure I can make it. I'll just go slow."

Driving into the pooled water, her heartbeat sped up. The water was deep. She continued forward. She shouldn't have tried this. It was foolishness. *God, please get me through this.*

She drove forward a few more feet. She was almost there. Just a bit farther. The car stalled.

She gasped, put the gear in Park, turned it off, and tried to start it again. Nothing. She pressed the side of her head against the window. The water seemed to be just below her car door. She could get out, but she'd have to leave her car. *God, what if it washes off the road and into the ditch?*

She rested her forehead against the steering wheel. *Which is why I shouldn't have tried to go across this in the first place.*

Ivy jumped at the sound of a knock on her windshield. She peered through the glass. Relief flooded her spirit when she saw Carter. She rolled down the window, and the rain pelted her shoulder and arm. He pointed to the ignition. "Put it in gear. I'll push you out of the puddle."

Unsure of the safety of his idea, but unwilling to argue with him, she shifted the gear into Drive. In her rearview mirror, she watched him lean forward and put his full weight into pushing the car forward. Guilt pounded her head as the car nudged forward. Once out of the puddle, he ran back to the window and she lowered it again. "We'll leave it here. Come with me. I'll take you where you need to go."

Before she could respond, he ran across the road to his van and drove it close to her car. Embarrassed, she lifted the raincoat hood over her head and jumped into the front seat of his van.

"So, where you going?"

Ivy looked at Carter. Drenched from head to toe, water dropped from the tip of his nose. His jaw tensed, and she could tell he'd spit the question through clenched teeth. He was mad. Probably because he was soaked clear to the bone. All because she'd foolishly decided to drive through a foot-high puddle. "I'm sorry you had to push me through that. You're soaked."

"Not a problem." He didn't look at her, but she noticed he gripped the steering wheel so tight his knuckles were white. "Where am I taking you?"

"The pantry."

"What?" He peered at her, his gaze every bit as angry as her mother's had been. "Why are you going to the pantry?"

She shrugged, feeling like a chastised schoolgirl. "It's Saturday. We stock on Saturdays."

He pointed outside. "In this weather? You felt it important to stock the pantry in this?"

She straightened her shoulders. He was right. She shouldn't have tried to get out in this. But it wasn't any of his business. He wasn't her father, her husband, or even her boyfriend. He had no say about what she did or didn't do. "Well, why are you out?"

"I have to work."

He clamped his lips shut and drove the few yards to the pantry. She appreciated that he parked as close as he could to the door.

He turned in his seat. "Look. I'm glad you're all right. Flash flooding can be very dangerous."

His voice had tendered, but his jaw was still set in frustration. She felt bad he'd have to work all day in soaked clothes. She pointed to his shirt. "I'm sorry. You're going to be miserable today."

His eyebrows raised, and he nodded. "Yes, but not because of these." He pulled at the wet shirt clinging to his well-formed muscles. "I've got extra clothes in the back."

She gazed into his eyes. They were so dark and deep, she couldn't help but wonder at the mysteries behind them. She loved a good mystery.

The set of his jaw shifted, and his expression changed. He reached up and brushed her cheek, and she gasped at the cold, wet touch. His eyes smoldered with intensity, and she knew if she leaned forward just slightly, she would feel his lips against hers.

Brent pulled up behind them, snapping her to reality. She leaned back, and Carter pursed his lips. "I'll come back to get you. What time?"

"We'll be done by noon."

He looked out the windshield. "I'll be back then."

She wanted to talk about what almost happened. She wanted to know if Carter felt the same toward her—if he struggled to close his eyes and not see her face. But he wasn't going to talk about it. Not now.

She could tell him that Brent would take her home. But she wanted him. Carter.

"Okay. See you then." She opened the van door then ran into the pantry.

Brent frowned. "Who was that?"

"Carter Smith, the dad of one of my students."

"Wasn't he the guy who paid back all the groceries?"

Ivy smiled. "Yeah. That's him."

"Why did he bring you to the pantry?"

"Did you see the car down the road? The one that looks like mine?"

"Yeah."

She pointed to her chest. "Mine. I tried to drive past the middle school."

He shook his head. "Oh Ivy."

"Didn't make it. He pushed me out of the way and drove me the rest of the way."

"That was nice of him."

"It was." She looked up at Brent. He wanted to talk more about it, but she had no intention of doing so. She walked toward the back. "Let's get started."

She heard him let out a loud sigh. He was the third person she'd exasperated today. Maybe if she stuck to counting vegetable cans and packages of flour and sugar, she'd get into less trouble.

Grabbing the inventory sheet, she set to work adding the cans of vegetables that had been donated the last week. Brent went to the office to work on figures. She was thankful to be alone. Gave her time to think.

She'd wanted to kiss Carter. It surprised her how much she wanted to kiss him. But he was completely wrong for her. Ready-made family. Unstable job.

Her mother had harped on her for a good hour after they'd run into the Smith family at the fast-food restaurant. Mom fussed that she'd seen something in his eyes. And she didn't like it one bit.

Ivy'd seen it today. It was a yearning that sent tingles down her spine. She hadn't thought much about wanting a husband until Mirela fell in love with Josif. Since then, she'd wondered when God would bring the right man into her life. Her mother's choice just didn't send the tingles to her toes that Carter had.

She looked in the direction of the office. Boy, it would be so much easier if she could fall for Brent. Stable job. No kids. Loved the Lord with passion. Everything she wanted in a man.

Yet, she couldn't get Carter Smith out of her mind. He was a Christian. She'd known it even before his mention of church the night at the restaurant. She could just tell. The way he acted with his kids and with other people. His faith shone through his words, through the way he carried himself and treated the kids.

She counted up the different vegetables and wrote their tallies on the sheet. Trying to stay busy, she added up the boxes of instant mashed potatoes and the cans of tuna and other canned meats. She was being too efficient, too fast.

Once finished, her brain shifted back to Carter. She wondered what it would have felt like to kiss him. She wanted to rake her fingers through his dark hair. Her heartbeat sped up at the idea.

"How's it going?"

She jumped at Brent's voice. Laughing nervously, she flattened the front of her shirt. "I've finished."

Fearing he could read her thoughts, she walked away from him and toward the desk. She squirted sanitizer in her hands and rubbed them together.

"You want me to take you home?" asked Brent, as he touched her elbow.

"That's okay. I'll take her."

Ivy jumped again and turned to see Carter standing in the doorway. Her heart pounded against her chest. She had lost her heart to him.

Chapter 9

The tall guy walked to Carter and extended his hand. "Name's Brent Connors. Nice to meet you."

Carter shook his hand. "Carter Smith."

The guy—Brent—shoved both hands in his front pockets. "Hey, that was terrific that you reimbursed the pantry. Not many patrons do that. 'Course, not many are able to."

Carter bit back the embarrassment swelling in his gut. He knew the voucher had been God's provision, but his flesh still reeled that he'd had to take a handout.

"So, where do you work?" asked Brent, as he pulled his hands out of his pockets and crossed his arms in front of his chest.

Carter sized up the man. Tall and thin, he still looked athletic. His tone, though friendly, held an underlying challenge. He was protective of Ivy.

"I work in construction. Had my own business. Economy hurt us, but business is starting to pick back up."

Brent nodded. "That's great." He motioned toward Ivy. "Don't worry about Ivy. I'll take her home."

"No. It's okay. I'll take her."

Ivy marched toward them, her eyes squinted and fists balled. "I believe I can speak for myself."

Carter grinned at the fire in her tone. She grabbed her purse off the table and pushed the strap high on her shoulder. She zeroed in on the tall guy. "Brent, Carter is going to take me. I need to talk with him."

Victory swelled within his gut. She wanted to go with him. Carter nodded to Brent. "Nice meeting you."

He followed Ivy out the door. The rain had stopped. The sun peeked through the clouds intermittently, as if toying with the notion of brightening the day. People were venturing from their houses, and though Ivy's car was parked on the side of the road, they needed to get it to a better location.

More than likely, it was the carburetor that stalled. He hoped it'd had time to dry and would start up. As he hopped into his van, he remembered she'd said she wanted to talk with him.

He hoped it had nothing to do with the fact that he'd almost kissed her before dropping her off. He'd spent most of the morning dropping tools and measuring wrong, thinking about her and what he'd almost done. One moment he berated himself for the feelings; the next he growled that he hadn't manned up and done it.

It had practically scared the life right out of him when he saw her car stalled in the foot of water. He'd known it was her. Remembered her car from when he'd loaded it with groceries the night of the home visits. He'd only seen one blue Toyota Corolla with a "Jesus Is Lord" sticker in the back window in Greenfield. He'd almost come unglued when he saw it in the road.

Pushing the queasiness that filled his gut to the side, he asked, "What did you want to talk about?"

"Let's check on my car first, if you don't mind."

He drove the short distance to her car and pulled up behind it. Just as he was about to offer to start it, she hopped out and raced to the car. Within moments, it revved to life, and she walked back to him. "Carburetor must have dried out."

He nodded, surprised that she would know what had probably happened. His mom would want to tan his hide for thinking such chauvinistic thoughts, but Ivy didn't look like the kind of girl who would know a car had a carburetor.

"Listen. I need to talk to you about Lauren."

Relief washed over him that she didn't want to discuss their almost kiss, followed by a wave of dread. Lauren perplexed him to no end. One minute she acted like a teenager; the next moment she behaved years younger than her age. She was more often mean to her brothers than not. And she had what he feared to be an unhealthy attachment to her teacher. Even though Carter had to admit he struggled with the same problem as well.

"Okay. What's going on?"

She looked at the road. "I hate to talk about it here. Do you have time to go get some lunch?"

Carter swallowed. He wasn't sure lunch was such a good idea. He was already fighting his growing attraction for Ivy. Spending time together would only encourage it. But he had to hear what she had to say about Lauren whether it was over lunch, on the phone, or at the school. "Sure. Where do you want to go?"

She shrugged. "Anywhere you like particularly?"

"You pick. I'll follow."

She grinned, and he watched her walk back to the car.

Again, he wished she hadn't been so nicely put together. Or at least, that he was blind to her cuteness.

He picked up his phone and pressed the button to call home to make sure all was well. Jocelyn answered the phone.

"How's it going?"

He cringed at the sound of yelling in the background. They didn't seem mad, but it was sure loud.

"Great. Fed them cereal. Watched a couple of programs on television. Now we're playing hide-and-seek."

He breathed a sigh of relief. The kids loved the game, and Gabe always got himself so tickled, he squealed through the whole thing. Never had any trouble finding Gabe.

"I was going to grab some lunch then I'll be home."

"No prob, dude. You want me to feed the munchkins?"

Carter grinned. From any other child, he would think she was being rude, but not Jocelyn. The teen was as genuine as a hard day's work and had a heart just as big. She was a lot like her mother, and Anna had been a godsend for his family more times than he could count since Mary's death. "That would be great. Do you know what you want to fix?"

"No worries." He envisioned her swatting her hand through the air. "I'll scrounge something together. I got your back."

"You got my back?"

"Yup."

"Jocelyn, what programs did you and the kids watch earlier?"

"Only stuff approved by you." She giggled. "Stop worrying, Carter. I know the rules. You know I've got this."

"Okay. Thanks, Jocelyn."

He clicked off the phone then turned into the restaurant's parking lot. It was one of those soup and sandwich places. Not his kind of eating. He liked a little more substance, but it would do.

Ivy got out of the car. The wind grabbed her hair and whipped it through the air. She was entirely too beautiful. It would take every ounce of strength to make it through this lunch. *God, I may need a bit of extra backing from You, too.*

"Is this place okay?"

He hopped out of the van and shoved his keys in his front pocket. "Sure."

"It's my favorite lunch place."

Now, that didn't surprise him. Her knowledge about carburetors was unexpected, but her liking froufrou restaurants for lunch didn't surprise him at all.

Ivy placed her soup and salad on the table and put the tray on top of the trash container. She sat across from Carter. She hadn't meant for him to pay for her lunch, but he'd insisted. And she felt a little weird about it. They weren't on a date, though she wouldn't have minded if they were. But she also worried about what he'd think regarding her concerns with Lauren.

"You want me to pray before we eat?"

"Absolutely."

Ivy bowed her head and kept her hands in her lap. Carter's voice was soft as he murmured thankfulness for their food. Her cheeks warmed when he thanked God for her being Lauren's teacher. Her heart twisted with more admiration for him when he petitioned God for help with Lauren. When he finished, Ivy opened her eyes and stared at her soup.

She'd fallen hard for this man. Before today, she knew she was attracted to him. But after he'd helped her with the car and now his sincere prayer—she'd simply lost all reservation about her feelings for him.

Forcing herself not to fall apart right in front of him, she took a bite of her salad.

"Tell me about Lauren."

Ivy looked up at him. He was tired. It was obvious being a single dad took its toll on him. She admired him all the more that he did such a good job juggling work, home, and three children. But the concern etching his brow weighed her heart. She wanted to touch his cheek and tell him everything would be all right.

God, give me the right words. She wiped her mouth with the napkin and stared back into his eyes. Her hands trembled and she placed them under the table in her lap. "First, I have to tell you that I love Lauren. I care about her, and…"

He waved his hand in a circular motion to speed her up. "Ivy, I know you're a very caring person. It's obvious. But what's going on?"

She relayed the incident that happened Friday with Roger then continued, "Lauren is very attached to me."

Carter's gaze fell to his plate. "I've noticed."

She reached across the table and touched his hand. "That's not a bad thing."

Realizing what she'd done, she pulled back her hand, grabbed her napkin, and scrunched it in her grasp.

"It is if she doesn't want you to help the other students."

Carter flexed the hand she had touched, and she hoped she hadn't offended him. Electricity had shot through her from the touch. Surely, he had felt the same.

Shaking the thought away, she reached in her purse and pulled out a piece of paper. "The first day of school Lauren mentioned she wanted to be a cheerleader."

Carter lifted his brows and nodded, as if he'd heard this before.

"I hope you don't mind, but I made a list of a few gymnastic places. There's only one in Greenfield, but there are a few others that aren't too far away." She pointed to the paper. "I called and found out the cost for lessons as well."

Carter furrowed his brow and took the paper from her. He studied it until Ivy found herself shifting in her chair. He looked back up at her. "You did all this for Lauren?"

She chuckled and took a bite of her salad. "It wasn't much, really. Just a few phone calls."

"Still, I…"

"Oh yeah, and I saw in the paper that the sign-ups for recreational cheerleading are this week and next week at the county park."

He studied her, and Ivy noticed her hands trembled when she brought the spoon to her lips for a sip of soup. She put the spoon down and wiped her hands with the napkin. He continued to stare at her, and she wondered if he was angry or felt as if she'd imposed.

Insecurity welled inside her. Why wouldn't the man speak? Say something.

"These are great ideas. I'll look into it. May be hard with my schedule…"

"I'll be glad to help if you need me."

Ivy bit her lip. She had such a big mouth. She didn't mind helping. Her love for Lauren was genuine, but she had no idea what Carter would think. He'd been perturbed with her suggestion to make her one of Lauren's emergency contacts—which he'd never done. Why would she think he would want her help with practices and ball games?

Carter narrowed his gaze. "Why?"

Ivy shrugged. "Why, what?"

"Why would you help me with gymnastics and cheer-leading?"

She blew out a breath. Just as she thought, he'd gotten offensive—like she wanted to steal his kids away from him. She was Lauren's teacher. Shouldn't she want to help the child? Finding herself frustrated with his pride, she lifted her hands in surrender. "Look. I didn't mean to offend you."

"You didn't offend me. But, why?"

She leaned forward. "Because sometimes we need a little help."

He pushed his plate away from him, sat back in his seat, and crossed his arms in front of his chest. "I don't need help."

"That sounds a whole lot like a little too much pride, if you ask me."

"Well, I don't."

"Fine." Ivy stood and grabbed her soup and salad off the table. She'd only eaten half her meal, but she wasn't hungry anymore. She peered down at Carter. "The offer still stands. For Lauren's sake."

She dumped her trash then marched to her car. Once inside, remorse and embarrassment flooded her. She'd never shifted from fighting attraction to complete frustration so quickly before. And she'd never behaved so unprofessionally with a parent. Her feelings for Carter and his children tainted how she responded to him.

Her cheeks flamed as she drove home. *God, I can't believe I acted like that. He has no idea how I feel for him, and he shouldn't. I can't believe I talked to the parent of a student in such a way.*

She pulled into the driveway, debating if she should call and apologize. Wondering if that would make it worse.

How would she explain herself? *I kinda like you and your family, so I went a little cuckoo at the restaurant.*

Her cheeks burned anew as she walked into the house. Her mom wrapped her in a hug. "I'm so glad you're safe."

She frowned at her mother. "What?"

"Brent told me about your stalled car and that Carter Smith drove you to get it, but that was more than an hour ago. What in the world have you been doing?"

Ivy bit back an angry retort. Brent had no right to call her mother. She was an adult. "I needed to speak with him concerning his daughter."

Her mother shifted her stance. "And that's all?"

Aggravation welled inside her and toppled over the frustration and embarrassment she felt regarding Carter. "What if it wasn't, Mom?"

Her mother shook her head. "Oh Ivy, don't tell me you have feelings for that man. You don't need…"

"Don't worry, Mom. The man has too much pride for me."

She didn't wait for her mother's response. She marched back to her bedroom and shut the door. Flopping onto the bed, she rested the back of her arm over her face. Maybe if she went back to sleep, she could wake up and start this day all over.

Chapter 10

Ivy plastered a smile to her face when she opened the door for Mirela and her family. Her sister took one look at her, lifted her right eyebrow, then handed Benny to Josif. She wrapped her arms around Ivy. "Are you okay, sis?"

Ivy released a long breath while Josif and the kids made their way into the kitchen. Her mother's excited tones while talking to Benny and Bella sounded from the room. Phil Mamry's voice boomed in greeting as well. Ivy swiped away tears that had suddenly welled in her eyes. "It's been quite a week."

Mirela still held her tight as she talked over Ivy's shoulder. "Does it have to do with what I see happening in the kitchen?"

Ivy nodded. "But that's only part of it." She pulled away from her sister and lifted her hand, making a small space between her thumb and index finger. "Only a tiny part of it, really."

"Okay. You go to your room. I'll go check on them in the kitchen. Once I know all is well, I'll tell Mom you need to show me something, and I'll come up."

Ivy grinned. Their mother, wonderful as she was in so many ways, nosed into both of their business more than either wished. If their mom had the slightest hint that Ivy had teared up, the whole family would have to know all of Ivy's thoughts, feelings, and quandaries. The whole family and Phil.

She scaled the steps and walked into her room. At twenty-six, she'd lived at home her entire life. And enjoyed it. Never saw a reason to move out. But lately, she felt squeezed and dependent.

Plopping onto her bed, she grabbed one of the decorative pillows and shoved it under both arms. She leaned forward and stared at her toenails. She needed a pedicure. Something she and Mirela often did together. But her sister was a married woman with kids now. And she lived forty-five minutes away.

"Spill it."

Ivy looked up and saw Mirela standing in the doorway. She held a can of Ivy's favorite soft drink in her right hand and tissues in the other. Attempting to grin at Mirela's familiar sister-to-the-rescue scene, another pang of sadness nailed her gut. "Don't need the tissues today. I've got to hold it together, so Mom doesn't suspect anything."

Mirela placed the tissues on the bed. "Just in case." She popped the can's top and handed it to Ivy. "What's going on?"

Ivy tried to put her finger on all that had her feeling so discombobulated. It was more than her mother's newfound relationship with Phil or her mom's matchmaking with Brent. So much had changed and was continuing to change. And Ivy was a woman of order. Consistency.

"Do you not like Phil?" asked Mirela.

"That's just the thing." Ivy tossed the throw pillow toward the top of the bed. "I wanted her to date Phil so that she'd get off my back about Brent."

"She's still trying to set you two up?"

Ivy nodded. "But I don't care *that* much. Mom's been trying to get Brent and me together for months." She picked at a frayed thread on the comforter. "I guess I didn't expect them to hit it off so well. And so fast."

"It's kinda weird, isn't it?"

"Very."

Mirela didn't respond at first, and Ivy wondered if her sister thought she was silly, selfish, or both.

"I think Dad would like Phil."

"I do, too."

"Maybe not so much if he were still alive."

Ivy glanced at her sister, spying the playful glint in her eyes. "I think you're right. Dad probably wouldn't like another guy hitting on his wife if he were around."

"But I think he'd want her to be happy. To have someone in her life—now that he's gone."

Ivy nodded. "It's not just Phil."

"I know."

She looked at Mirela, a natural beauty with her dark hair, eyes, and always tanned skin. She sat at the end of the bed, her legs crossed in a pretzel, just as she'd done for nearly all the years of their lives. "I miss you."

"I miss you, too. Being a newlywed is wonderful but different. And adding the children so soon...I love them, but there are days I want nothing more than to drive to Greenfield and hang out with my sister."

"They seem to be adjusting well. I knew Benny would, since he's still a toddler and you'd watched him from six weeks old, but Bella seems to love being part of the family, also."

Mirela tightened her ponytail as she nodded. "She has adjusted well, but she's a little behind in school, and she worries a lot that I'll leave her like her mom did."

Ivy thought of Lauren. The girl had driven her past exhaustion the last week. She didn't want to play at recess—only sit by Ivy. She asked questions to problems that Ivy knew she understood—simply to have a reason to raise her hand or walk to Ivy's desk. Ivy tried sitting her by Rachel, a girl Lauren liked. It didn't work. She tried partnering her with a student who needed extra help in reading, but Lauren hadn't been interested in helping the child.

Ivy neared her wit's end. Lauren needed an outlet. She'd tried to inadvertently find out if Carter had ever started the girl in gymnastics or cheerleading, but as far as she could figure, he hadn't signed Lauren up for either.

"Girls, what are you doing up there? Supper is almost ready," yelled their mother.

Ivy sighed. She'd wanted to talk with Mirela about Lauren. And Carter.

Mirela patted Ivy's leg. "Before I leave, we're planning a pedicure date."

Ivy followed her sister down the stairs. "I definitely need one."

They walked into the dining room, and Ivy sucked in her breath. Brent sat at the table beside Josif. The two were deep in conversation about the Tennessee football team. Ivy glared at her mother.

Her mom's lips lifted into a smile that reminded her of the Grinch. "Come on in, girls. Have a seat."

Ivy knew her mom meant for her to sit by Brent, but for spite she plopped in the chair beside Bella. She unfolded her napkin and placed it in her lap before her mother could protest. Her mom could sit by the man she determined to invite to every meal possible.

She knew her sister held back from laughing out loud as she sat in the chair beside Benny's highchair. Mirela winked and offered a single nod, agreeing with Ivy's act of rebellion.

"Ivy, it's good to see you."

Brent's sincere, sweet tone shamed Ivy, and she rallied up the desire to be nice to the man. It wasn't his fault her mom wouldn't let up.

"Nice to see you, too, Brent."

"I was worried about you last Saturday. Made me nervous—you taking a ride from that Carter Smith guy—since we don't really know him. You never answered my texts."

Ivy's cheeks burned. Talk about calling a girl out on her shortcomings. And right in front of everyone. She hadn't responded for a reason. She didn't want to lead him on. And, it was not his business or place to decide who she should and should not be taking rides from.

"Sorry 'bout that," she mumbled then glanced at her sister.

"Yes. I had to text Brent to let him know you'd made it home safely," said her mother.

"Well, I did lie down when I got home. Had quite a headache."

Mirela's eyebrows raised, and Ivy knew she wanted the lowdown on Carter Smith. She'd happily tell her sister every sordid detail, if they could spend any time together. She needed advice.

Her heart felt at peace every time she was near the Smith family. Any of them. She remembered little Gabe resting his head on her shoulder, wrapping his chubby fingers around strands of her hair. She'd practically melted into the ground from his sweetness.

And Carter. Her heart beat a staccato rhythm, sending her into breathless pants, at the thought of him. Her reaction to seeing or talking to him was stronger than anything she'd experienced before.

Her mother continued, "But when you woke up, the polite thing to do would have been to return Brent's texts."

Fury welled within her. She was old enough to make her own choices, and if she were rude to someone and her mother felt the need to point that out, she did not need to do so at a dinner table full of guests. Her mother would find her exceptionally rude when she walked out of this dinner, which she planned to do this instant. She placed her napkin on the table and started to stand.

"Why don't we say grace? I'm famished."

Ivy paused and glanced at Phil. She didn't want to upset everyone, especially not the kids. She smiled, thankful that he'd taken the focus away from her. He winked, and she wondered if the man might be an ally in stopping her mother's matchmaking. At the very least, he could be a distraction.

Grabbing the napkin off the tabletop, she twisted it in her lap. No more trying to manipulate things, especially when it came to Phil Mamry. No more trying to run from things, especially when it came to Brent Connors. And no more being forced into situations, especially when it came to her mother. Open, upfront, but kind, honesty would be her new motto.

She listened to Phil's prayer and offered a quiet *amen* when he finished. They passed the food around the table. Ivy speared a small lemon chicken breast and placed it on Bella's plate then got another small one for herself.

Bella brushed strands of hair away from her face then

grabbed a roll from the bowl in front of her. Ivy pushed back thoughts of how many germs traveled in one's hair.

"Gammy and Aunt Ivy, I got an A on my spelling test," proclaimed Bella.

Her mother squealed with delight, everyone at the table clapped, and Ivy wrapped her arm around Bella's shoulder and squeezed. "Good job."

"She worked hard. Studied for three nights," said Mirela.

Ivy knew that meant Mirela had studied hard as well. Pride and marvel washed over her anew that her sister had taken on a family the same year she married.

Carter traipsed through her mind. If she ever married him, she'd have three children from the moment she said the vows. The idea seemed impossible, yet her spirit challenged that God was the Creator of making the impossible possible.

"Ivy, I have an extra ticket for next Saturday's football game."

Ivy blinked, forcing her mind back to the dinner with her family and Brent. "I'm sorry. What?"

"Would you like to go with me?"

Ivy stared at the man who had been her friend for several years. She didn't want things to change between them. Fury at her mother swelled within her. If Mom had left him alone, his feelings for her would have never shifted.

"Of course she'll go," said her mother.

Ivy stood and smacked her napkin on the table. She focused on Brent. "I'm sorry. I have plans that day." She looked around the table. "Excuse me."

Her mother started to retort, but Ivy walked to the bathroom and shut the door. Placing her hands on the sink, she stared at her reflection. *God, please help me with my mother. I know I am to honor her, but she is making it very difficult.*

She closed her eyes and tilted back her head. Working at the food pantry had been a passion for a long time. Brent was a wonderful man, but she didn't feel for him as a woman should for a mate. And she didn't need this added stress as she tried to decipher what was going on with her heart and emotions when it came to Carter.

She turned on the faucet then splashed cool water in her face. She pressed the towel against her. *And tell me what to say to Brent.*

Carter pressed his fingers against his temple. "Practices are Tuesdays and Thursdays at four o'clock?"

"I know it's kind of an early time," the coach of Lauren's recreational cheerleading squad responded. She sounded like she was all of eighteen. If *that* old. "But it was the only time we could get the cafeteria for practices."

Carter took in his seven-year-old daughter, jumping around the house like someone had set fire to her blue jeans. If only he hadn't asked her to answer the phone. She wouldn't have known it was her cheerleading coach who called. He could have told her cheerleading hadn't worked out and that she'd just have to be content with gymnastics lessons.

He wouldn't have lied to her. The truth was, even though she knew her coach was on the phone, those practice times did not work. He didn't get home until five. And he couldn't ask Anna to take her. The woman babysat six kids every day.

"I'll have to give you a call back," Carter said, trying to hold back a growl.

"No need. I'll see her Tuesday."

The line went dead, and Carter pushed the Off button

on his phone. Carter sat on the ottoman and patted beside him. "Lauren, come here."

She barreled into him, wrapping her arms around his neck. "Thank you so much, Daddy. I'm going to be a cheerleader like Rachel."

He detached her arms from his neck and sat her beside him. Everything in him didn't want to disappoint her. But he would have to do it. "Lauren, listen. I'm still working at four o'clock."

She shrugged, her eyes still sparkling with excitement. "That's okay."

"Honey, that's your practice time."

"So?"

She didn't understand, and he dreaded the look of sadness that would wrap her face once she did. "I can't take you to practices."

"Then I'll just go to games."

He shook his head. "No, honey. You won't know the cheers." He sucked in his breath, preparing himself for her disappointment. "You're not going to be able to do it."

"What?" Lauren jumped off the ottoman. "Daddy, you said I could. You promised. Miss Adams will take me. She said she would."

"Lauren, we are not asking Miss Adams."

"Please, Daddy," Lauren cried. Tears streamed down both her cheeks. "You said…"

"I can't help what I said. There's nothing I can do."

"Yes, there is. You just won't."

She ran to her room and shut the door, harder than she should have, but Carter decided to let her have her cry. He didn't blame her that she was upset.

Gabe tugged at his shirt. "I be a cheerweader, Daddy."

He knew Lauren had been practicing cheers she'd conjured up with her brothers. Picking up his youngest child,

Carter spied Clay on the far end of the couch. Tears welled in his second child's eyes. Carter frowned. "What's the matter, buddy?"

"You said she could be a cheerleader."

Clay hopped off the couch, moped to his room, and shut the door. Carter walked to Gabe's room to change his diaper. Trying to keep his heart from breaking in two, he laid the boy on the changing table. Gabe's legs sprawled past the edge. He was way too big for it. If Mary were here, Gabe would have been potty trained.

But she's not here. And it's not my fault that I can't get Lauren to those practices. God, I feel like I'm carrying the weight of the world on my shoulders. I can't do it all.

"You're right you can't. You need help."

Lauren's begging to ask Miss Adams traipsed through his mind. He remembered their lunch when Ivy offered to help out with practices or ball games. He didn't want to ask her. Seeing her caused him physical pain. The last time he'd been so attracted to a woman had been more than a decade ago with Mary.

But it wasn't about him. It was about his children. He'd have to suffer through it. Take sleeping aids or cold showers to get Ivy out of his mind at night. Avoid her when he could. Have her drop Lauren off and leave. He would pick her up when practice was over. He'd have to do it. For Lauren.

With Gabe changed, he lifted the boy off the changer and set him on his feet. Gabe raced to his brother's room. Carter made his way to Lauren's. He knocked on the door then opened it. She lay facedown on her bed, her back still heaving.

He sat beside her and touched her back. Seeing her so upset hurt worse than a hammer strike to his thumb. "Lis-

ten, sweetie, I said you could be a cheerleader, and I'm
going to try to work it out."

Lauren sat up and swiped her eyes with the back of
her hand. A smile brightened her red-streaked, swollen
face. "Really?"

Carter nodded. "I'm gonna try."

Lauren wrapped her arms around his neck. "Thank
you, Daddy."

Carter welcomed the hug. He kissed the top of her head.
"Now, go practice your cheers with your brothers while
I fix supper."

"Okay."

As Lauren ran to Clay's room, Carter walked to the
kitchen. Beef stew already simmered in the slow cooker.
All he needed to do was butter some bread and set the
table. Nausea stirred within him at the thought of asking
Ivy's help. Somehow, he'd have to do it.

Chapter 11

Ivy stood at the door of the classroom and welcomed in the students. Lauren ran down the hall, her backpack bouncing from side to side. She held out a paper. "I've got something for you, Miss Adams."

She took the letter. "Thank you."

Lauren panted. She bent over and put her hands on her knees to catch her breath. Ivy helped her take off the backpack and patted her back.

Lauren grinned. "It's from Daddy. He wants you to take me to cheerleading practice."

Taken aback, Ivy opened the letter. It only said he wanted to add Ivy to the emergency list and requested she'd bring her home that day. After their last encounter over lunch, she was surprised he'd ask to add her to the list. He'd been unwilling to accept any offer of help, acting accusatory regarding her motives. In truth, she knew her feelings for Carter's children ran deep.

She cared about the trio, praying for them with more fervor than any of the children she taught. That didn't make her motives bad. Probably made her foolish, since she'd lost her heart to them and when the school year ended, she wouldn't see them anymore.

She motioned toward Lauren's chair. "Thank you. Go have a seat."

"I have a special delivery for Miss Adams."

Ivy turned and saw the school secretary holding an elaborate bouquet of flowers. "Oh my."

Ivy reached for the vase, but the petite secretary couldn't see over the flowers and leaves. "I'll just go put them on your desk. Didn't know it was your birthday."

"It's your birthday?" yelled Roger.

Ivy nodded. "As a matter of fact, it is."

"My birthday's in May," offered one of the students.

"Mine's in January."

"Miss Adams, did you know my birthday is in two weeks?" asked Lauren.

Ivy nodded and pointed to the bulletin board. "Yes. Your name is on the calendar. In fact, look up there. My name is under today's date."

The class responded with a collective "Oh."

"We gotta sing 'Happy Birthday,' " said Lauren. She stood and waved her hands like a conductor while the class and the elderly secretary sang to her.

Ivy's heart swelled when the students attacked her in a group hug. The secretary waved her good-bye, and Ivy looked at the enormous bouquet of mixed red and pink flowers. Her stomach churned at the thought of who would have sent the arrangement. She prayed it was her mother, though she doubted her mom would send her flowers. Settling the students back into their seats, she pulled the card off the prong. Just as she thought. Not her mother. Brent.

"Who are the flowers from?" asked Rachel.

Ivy placed the card back on the prong. "From a friend. Now class, get out your morning workbooks."

"Is it your boyfriend?" asked Roger.

Lauren threw a piece of paper at him. "Miss Adams doesn't have a boyfriend."

Ivy cleared her throat. "Lauren, that is not appropriate behavior. Pick up that paper and apologize to Roger."

Lauren stomped toward Roger's desk. He flinched as she retrieved the paper from the floor, apologized, then threw it away. She marched back to her seat and flopped down in a huff.

Ivy looked at Roger. "No. Just a friend." She turned her attention to the whole class. "Thank you for singing to me, but it is time to get started with our schoolwork."

She tried to focus on her students, but her gaze kept wandering to the clock. As soon as the class left for gym, she would call Brent and talk to him about the depth of their relationship. Her mother had given him the wrong impression, and it wasn't fair for him to feel they had some kind of romantic future. She cringed when she thought of the card reading "Love, Brent."

If Carter hadn't asked her to take Lauren home, she would have stopped by his office after school and talked to him face-to-face. But now she didn't know how long she would be at Lauren's, and she had already planned to meet Mirela, Josif, and the kids for dinner. Mom had to work, which was likely a blessing, or she may have been having dinner with Brent again.

Ten o'clock finally arrived, and Ivy walked the students to the gymnasium. Not wanting anyone to hear the conversation, she walked out the front door and stood by the flagpole. The school set on the outskirts of town. Mountains and hills billowed around her on three sides. With the beginning of autumn, a touch of coolness nipped the air. The wind whipped her hair, and she breathed in the scent of nature. Dialing the number, she asked God for guidance about what to say.

"Good morning. This is Brent Connors. How can I help you?"

Ivy wavered at the cheerful sound of his voice. She didn't want to hurt his feelings, and that flower arrangement had to have cost him a bundle.

"Hello?" He spoke again. "If you're nervous about talking with someone, I understand."

Ivy swallowed the knot in her throat. He thought she needed advice regarding an unplanned pregnancy, which would be the case for most people who called a pro-life counseling agency. Temptation to hang up and wait a few days swelled within her, and she reached up to push the Off button.

She shook her head. No. She needed to do this. It wasn't fair to him. "Hi, Brent. It's Ivy."

"Ivy!" The cheerfulness returned. "Happy birthday. Did you get my flowers?"

"Yes. I did. Thank you. They're beautiful. But I need to talk to you."

"Absolutely." His chair squeaked, and she wondered if he'd sat down or stood up. "I planned to call you anyway. To see if you have plans for dinner."

"No. I mean, yes. I have plans with Mirela and her family." Ivy blinked and wrapped one arm around the flagpole. She needed it to hold her up on her trembling legs.

Disappointment laced his words. "That's too bad. Thought I'd treat you for your birthday."

She had to do this. Just open her mouth and spill it, as Mirela would say. "Listen, Brent. You're my friend."

"I know I'm your friend." His chair squeaked again.

"But I thought, well, maybe we could see if we wanted to be more."

"I don't want to be more."

There she'd said it. Straightforward. Point-blank. Silence pounded from her phone, and Ivy felt a headache coming on. "Brent, are you there?"

"I'm here."

"I don't want to hurt your feelings." She released the flagpole and twirled a strand of hair between her fingers. "I really want us to be friends."

"You know, I read somewhere that guys and girls can't be friends, and it's usually the guy who wants more."

Ivy bit her bottom lip. She didn't know what to say. She begged God for direction, but He didn't give any hints, so she stayed quiet.

"I'll see you at the food pantry on Saturday." The cheerfulness in his voice had gone. Frustration had taken its place.

"I'm sorry, Brent. The flowers *are* beautiful."

"You're welcome for them. And I'm glad you were honest."

The line disconnected, and Ivy pulled the phone away from her ear. Her stomach ached from hurting Brent's feelings. She leaned against the flagpole then lowered herself until she sat on the concrete foundation. Breaking up with a guy who wasn't really her boyfriend was not what she'd planned for her birthday.

Her cell phone beeped at an incoming text message. It was from Mirela. She opened it. Bella sick with fever. Have to cancel : (Happy Birthday.

Well, the day couldn't get much better, now could it?

An alarm screamed from inside the building. She looked at the time on her phone. She'd forgotten to pick up her class early from gym for the practice fire drill. Racing to the front door, she yanked on it. Locked. Pressing her head against the glass, she closed her eyes. *God, this day is only getting worse.*

Carter looked at his watch for what seemed the hundredth time. Lauren had called and told him Miss Adams had a teacher meeting after school and she wouldn't bring her home until after four-thirty. He paced the floor. *What was I thinking? The woman could have had any number of plans, and I just send her a note without warning to bring my kid home from school.*

He was a heel. No. He was the lint-covered, pebble-ridden glob of gum on the bottom of his heel. "Where Lauren, Daddy?" asked Gabe.

Bending over, he ruffled his son's hair. "She'll be home soon."

He scratched his jaw then raked his fingers through his hair. He'd even left the worksite early today so he could meet Ivy at the house right after school.

"Daddy, I'm hungry." Clay walked into the living room and hopped onto the leather recliner.

Carter had planned to cook but had gotten himself so worked up about seeing Ivy and asking for her help with Lauren's practices that he simply didn't have it in him. "How 'bout I order us a couple pizzas?"

Clay pumped his fist through the air. "Yes."

Carter rolled through the numbers on his phone until he found the pizza place that delivered. He called and ordered two larges. If Ivy and Lauren didn't get here soon, he'd have to invite Ivy to stay for dinner. The thought excited and sickened him.

"I'm home!" The front door flew open, and Lauren bounded inside. "It's Miss Adams's birthday, so they had cake after school for her."

"I want cake." Clay stuck out his lower lip.

"I don't have any more." Lauren opened her hands then ran to her bedroom.

Ivy walked up the steps, and Carter opened the door for her. "I hear today is your birthday."

She smiled, but she seemed more tired than he'd ever seen her. "It is."

"Well, happy birthday."

"Thanks."

He motioned for her to have a seat on the couch. She looked beautiful in a dark skirt and light blue top. Her eyes sparkled to complement the shirt. "First, I need to apologize for not asking you if you were able to bring Lauren home today."

Ivy swatted the air. "No problem."

The boys ran into the room, and Clay hopped onto the couch beside Ivy, while Gabe started to climb in her lap. "Guys, Miss Adams is our guest. You can't just jump on top of her."

Ivy turned Gabe around to sit facing forward then she wrapped her arm around Clay's shoulder. "It's okay."

Carter's heart constricted. It wasn't okay. His boys had only seen her a few times and they were already cuddling up to her like she was their long-lost relative. It pained him. He already fought his attraction for her. He didn't need his kids falling for her as well. He couldn't do that to Mary.

Trying to think of something to take his mind off the maternal expression on her face, he asked, "So, how old are you?" He furrowed his brow. "I can't believe I just said that."

Ivy laughed. "Twenty-seven. Thought I'd be married with a couple of rugrats like these two by now." She cuddled his kids closer to her. "But God hasn't brought along the man…"

Her cheeks and neck darkened when their gazes met. His chest tightened, and he shuffled in his seat. He had to change the subject and quick. "I wanted to ask you about Lauren's practices."

"She mentioned you did."

"I wondered if you could keep her after school on Tuesdays and Thursdays until four o'clock. Her cheerleading practices start at that time in the cafeteria. You wouldn't have to stay with her. I'd pick her up when practice ended."

"Not a problem. I'd love to help."

Clay reached up and touched her hair, while Gabe leaned against her chest sucking his thumb. Carter couldn't take it anymore. He stood up and pulled the boys away from Ivy. "Go check on your sister."

They whimpered then scampered down the hall after Lauren. Carter sat back in the chair and realized that may not have been the best of plans. Now, he sat in the living room alone with his greatest temptation.

His heartbeat sped up as she smoothed out her skirt and shirt where the boys had ruffled them. She grabbed the bulk of her hair in one hand and swept it across one shoulder. Carter rubbed his hands together. He needed something to do besides just watch her.

She looked at him, and he couldn't believe how comfortable she seemed in his presence. He felt as though he battled an unseen magnetic field.

"Your boys are so sweet."

He laughed inwardly. Maybe that was how he could break the spell she had on him. Give her a little time with all three kiddos, watch her run for home, and confirm that she had no business in the Smith family's day-in-day-out life.

"Thanks. How's Lauren doing at school?"

"Still pretty clingy."

"I was afraid of that."

"I think having an outlet like cheerleading is going to help her. She really seems to want a woman in her life."

Ivy's cheeks tinged again, and Carter exhaled a long breath. "Probably because she had a terrific mother the first five years of her life. Now, she's stuck with me and the boys."

"You don't seem to be too bad."

The heaviness in Carter's chest lifted at her lighthearted response. She leaned forward in the chair. "You wanna tell me about your wife?"

No. Yes. Carter battled the guilt and frustration warring within him. "She looked a bit like you."

"Me?" Ivy placed her hand on her chest and leaned back.

"Well, your coloring. Blond hair. Blue eyes. She was a couple years older than you." He sat back in the chair. Something inside him snapped, and he shared about Mary. How she took care of him, the kids, and the house like it was a military operation. She ran a tight ship, cooked a killer meal, and loved them with every ounce of her being.

The doorbell rang, and Carter hopped out of the chair. Ivy stood as well. "You have company. I'd better be going."

Carter shook his head. "It's the pizza guy."

Clay ran into the room screaming, "Pizza!"

Gabe raced after him, and Lauren walked behind him. Carter paid the delivery kid. He turned and realized Lauren held a bag in her hand. "Will you stay and have pizza with us, Miss Adams?"

"No. No. I'd better be going."

Ivy grabbed her purse off the end table and lifted it over her shoulder. Carter realized he wanted her to stay. He'd opened up to her about Mary in a way he'd never done with anyone else before. She'd listened, receptive to his happiness and regrets. "If you don't have plans, I'd love for you to stay."

He wanted to be near her. It was her turn to share about herself.

Ivy put her purse down again. "Well, my sister did bail on me since my niece was sick, and my mom is working."

"What about your friend?" asked Lauren.

"My friend?"

"The one who sent you the flowers."

His chest tightened. Ivy looked at him. He determined not to be concerned or even curious about the friend who'd sent her flowers at school. He wondered if they were from the tall guy at the pantry. Not that it was any of his business or that he should even care.

Ivy shook her head as she studied him. "No. I'm not having dinner with my friend either."

"Good. You can stay with us." Lauren pulled out a chair.

Ivy sat down. Clay jumped onto the seat on one side of her and Lauren sat on the other. Carter took slow breaths, reminding himself it didn't matter who sent her flowers. He grabbed plates off the shelf and turned toward the table. His chest constricted again. It had been two years since five people sat at the table. And Ivy seemed to fit in perfectly.

"Before we eat, open your present." Lauren pushed the bag in front of Ivy.

"Okay." She unfolded the flaps, reached inside, and pulled out one of Gabe's building blocks. Then a super hero figure from Clay. Last, she pulled out a piece of construction paper.

Carter looked down at his daughter's artwork. She'd cut out hearts and flowers and glued them in various places. But the picture was their house and standing beside it was all five of them with their names written below, "Dad,

Miss Adams, Lauren, Clay, Gabe." At the top, she'd titled it "My Family."

"Thank you so much. These are wonderful presents. I love your picture, Lauren."

Nausea washed over Carter. He walked to the refrigerator and opened it to hold on to the door. Praying for God's strength, he took out soft drinks and juice boxes.

Had Lauren already forgotten her mother? Gabe would never remember her. For Clay, it was also unlikely. But he'd always hoped—prayed—that Lauren would have memories of her mom. Mary was a good mother. She deserved to be remembered.

Trying to act normal, he placed drinks on the table. He could feel Ivy's gaze on him. She was a nice woman. Super sweet. He appreciated all she was willing to do for Lauren. And it was nice the boys liked her, too. But he'd pledged his life to Mary. For better or worse. In sickness and health. He'd be sure to keep those vows at the forefront of his mind when he was around Ivy Adams.

"Till death do you part."

The Spirit nudged him, but her death was his fault. He couldn't forgive himself, and he couldn't give her up.

Chapter 12

Ivy watched as her mother waddled out of the nail salon with cotton still laced between her toes to keep them separated while they dried. She held her purse in one hand and her shoes in the other. Phil hopped out of the cab of the truck when he saw her, a smile bowing his mouth. He opened the door and helped her inside then they drove away.

"He's sweet to her, huh?"

Ivy looked at her sister. The salon chair's back massager pushed Mirela forward and backward.

"Really sweet."

Ivy leaned back in her chair and allowed the massager to work into her muscles. She'd needed this day out with her mom and sister. Though she hated to admit it, she was glad it was just her and Mirela now.

It had been two weeks since she'd spent her birthday with Carter and the children. She kept the picture Lauren had drawn in her dresser drawer. Each day she looked at it. Ivy had lost her heart to Carter that night. Completely.

The man's tender compassion and memories about his wife stirred a desire to know him on a deeper level. No longer was it just his muscles or dark eyes or even the nice way he treated his kids. It was the core of him she loved.

Carter made a promise and kept it. He didn't play games or try to make things work to his benefit. When he loved, it was selfless and honest and pure.

But he'd avoided her since that night. She took Lauren to practice, waited for Carter to get there, and then she left. Twice a week they exchanged pleasantries. But that was it. He'd built up a wall with a seemingly sole purpose of keeping her out.

"So, you gonna tell me about this guy already?" asked Mirela.

Ivy grinned. She didn't have to look at her sister to know she studied Ivy. "What do you want to know?"

"Everything." Mirela plopped the magazine she'd been flipping through onto the table between them. "Mom told me you ditched Brent once and for all."

Ivy winced. She hadn't wanted to hurt Brent, and the past two weeks at the pantry had been strained. In time, she hoped they wouldn't feel so awkward around each other. "Mom's the cause of that."

"Oh, I know. I think she knows it, too."

Ivy glanced at her sister. "She said that to you?"

Mirela nodded. "Now she's worried about this other guy."

Ivy leaned back in the chair. The lady giving the pedicure lifted a bottle of pink nail polish, and Ivy confirmed it was the color she'd wanted. She turned toward Mirela. "His name is Carter Smith, and I love him."

Mirela's eyebrows rose. "Whoa. Now, that's a statement."

Ivy wrinkled her nose. "I know, and yet, it's the complete truth. I love his kids, too."

"How many kids?"

"Three."

"No wonder Mom is worried."

Mirela's polish was finished, and the lady moved her to the table with a dryer for hands and feet. Ivy pondered Mirela's words while her technician finished. It was overwhelming to think about a man with a ready-made family, but she cared about them so deeply. Prayed for them daily. The few times she'd spent with them felt right.

When her polish was finished, Ivy moved to sit across from her sister. Mirela clasped her hands and rested them on top of the table. "I want to tell you what my week has been like. I've slept maybe two nights all the way through. Bella got over her fever but then picked up a stomach bug. I spent a day cleaning up after her, washing sheets and clothes, bathing Bella, making her soup. Then Benny got it, and I got sick with him."

Mirela's expression exhibited true concern and deep fatigue. "Ivy, I have never been so tired in my life. Are you sure it's not compassion you're feeling? You've always had a heart of gold, and—"

Ivy lifted her hand to stop Mirela. She'd heard this lecture from her mother. If God brought Carter Smith with three kids into her life, she would not argue. "If it is God's will, then…"

Mirela nodded. "If it is God's will, then we'll throw you a wedding today."

Ivy's heartbeat raced as she envisioned herself standing at an altar in a simple white wedding gown. Carter, in a classic black tux, stood across from her with Lauren,

Clay, and Gabe beside him, wearing a white dress and black tuxes.

"I've thought about this, Mirela. Prayed about it. You know I am not an irrational person. I'm orderly and cautious, almost to a fault."

Mirela rested her cheek against her fist. "You're right. But something is still worrying you."

"He loves his wife. It's like he blames himself for her death, and he won't allow himself to stop loving her."

"Does he have to stop loving her?"

Ivy blinked at Mirela's question. Did he? Could he love Mary and still love her the way she needed to be loved, with the same complete devotion he'd felt for Mary?

"Haven't you seen me love Mom with all that's in me and still love the mother who died when I was young?"

"Well, yes, but mother-daughter love is very different from the love between a husband and wife. A husband and wife become one in mind, body, and spirit. Mothers and daughters don't do that."

"You're right, but look at Mom. Do you think she no longer loves Dad?"

Ivy rolled her eyes. "Of course, she loves Dad."

Two women joined them at the table, and Ivy and Mirela stopped talking. Ivy tried to wrap her mind around what Mirela was saying.

She leaned over and touched her toes with the back of her finger. They were dry. They paid the technician and walked to the car. Mirela placed her hands on the hood. "Do you understand what I'm trying to say?"

Ivy shook her head. "I don't."

"Mom still loves Dad. She always will. They had a good marriage, raised two daughters. They were truly in love. Now, she's falling for Phil. Don't you think God's made her heart big enough to love him as well?"

Mirela got in the car, and Ivy did the same. They rode in silence back to the house. Mirela's words turned and twisted through Ivy's mind. It did make sense, and she wouldn't want Carter to forget the love he felt for Mary. His faithfulness to her was one of the reasons Ivy had fallen in love with him.

They pulled into the driveway. Mirela walked into the house while Ivy checked the mailbox. She spied a small letter addressed to her, written in a child's handwriting. Without a stamp or a return address, the sender must have dropped it in the mailbox while they were gone. Opening it, she discovered a birthday party invitation for the following day from Lauren. The child had written "Please Come" in huge letters on the left side.

Her cell phone beeped and Ivy dug it out of her front pocket then pushed the button to read the text message. Lauren is driving me crazy. Let me know if you are coming to the party.

She smiled. It was from Carter. She texted back. Wouldn't miss it for the world.

"She wouldn't miss it for the world," Carter said to Gabe as he changed his son into a clean pair of jeans and shirt. In less than half an hour, he'd have eight little girls in the house playing pin the tail on the donkey, hot potato, and whatever other games the girls wanted to play. And Ivy would be here.

He'd gladly add eight additional little girls if they could replace Ivy. The woman no longer haunted him—she overpowered him. It was all he could do to be civil when he picked Lauren up from her practices on Tuesdays and Thursdays.

Not only had Ivy taken over his thoughts, but Carter

seemed to be on the outs with God lately. And it hurt him to the core.

"Happy birthday!" Ivy's voice flowed down the hallway and into Gabe's room, sending shivers down Carter's neck.

"You're here!" Lauren squealed, and Carter heard her race to the front door. The boys followed.

He sucked in a few quick breaths. He could do this. He could practically build an entire house by himself. He could stand a few hours in Ivy's presence.

He walked down the hall. She stood in the door, holding Gabe on her hip. Her face shone with delight, her long blond hair flowing down one shoulder. He couldn't do it.

Nodding an acknowledgment to her, he turned on his heels and walked into the kitchen. Princess-themed cake sat on the table. Ice cream in the freezer. Plate, napkins, cups all placed on the table. Everything was ready.

"You need any help?"

She stood behind him. Just a few feet away. In the kitchen's doorway. He smelled her perfume, a light, inviting scent. He had to talk to her. His mother would be appalled if he didn't. He turned and shoved his hands in his front pockets. "Nope. Think I'm good."

She lifted up the bag in her hand. "I brought makeup and nail polish if the girls want me to fix them up."

Lauren stood beside her. How long she'd been there, he wasn't sure. He'd been focused on not saying or doing anything stupid in front of Ivy. "Oh Daddy, can we? Please?"

"That's fine with me."

Lauren clapped her hands then ran out of the kitchen, leaving him alone with Ivy. The last time this happened he'd spilled his heart out to her. He'd thought it would make her run, make the feelings he had go away. But it hadn't. If anything, his fixation with her had grown worse.

She walked toward him and looked at the table. "What a fun cake. Did you or Lauren pick it out?"

"Clay did."

"Smart boy. Knows what a girl likes."

She giggled, and Carter took a step around the table, away from her. He fixed the plates and napkins. Anything to keep his hands busy.

"Lauren has been doing so much better since she started cheerleading," Ivy offered.

Carter nodded. "She seems to be at home as well."

"I think she just needed an outlet. Something besides just school and home."

"Yep."

The doorbell rang, and Carter sighed in relief as he walked to the front door to greet two of Lauren's friends. The girls squealed and ran back to Lauren's room. Gabe hustled behind them.

"Are they all gonna scream like that, Daddy?" asked Clay.

"'Fraid so, son."

Clay rolled his eyes, hopped onto the couch, and covered his ears. "Gonna be a long night."

He said it, and Carter agreed. From the mouths of babes. Carter glanced over to see Ivy covering her mouth with her hand to keep from laughing at Clay.

The rest of the girls arrived over the next few minutes. Each squealed then ran into the room after Lauren. He glanced up at the clock. Two hours was all he had to endure.

Lauren flew back into the living room and grabbed Ivy's hand. "Can we do makeovers now?"

"We can, and we shall."

Carter watched as Ivy made her way back to Lauren's room. Though challenging for him, it was good Ivy had come to the party. She knew what girls liked. Though things were getting better, Lauren remained a mystery to him.

Several minutes passed, and he'd heard almost no noise from the room. He looked at the games he'd gotten out and wondered if they wouldn't want to play them.

"Can I watch TV, Daddy?" asked Clay.

Carter shrugged. He didn't see why not. Ivy had the girls and Gabe occupied in the room. He turned on a cartoon station and settled in beside his son.

Several more minutes passed. He looked up at the clock. Only an hour remained until the girls' parents would pick them up, and they still hadn't eaten cake or opened presents.

I better check on them. He stood and walked to Lauren's bedroom. The door was partly closed, but he could still see them all sitting on the floor in a circle. Each of the girls wore makeup on her face. He noticed they had various colors on their finger and toenails. Ivy was on her knees behind one of the girls, knotting the girl's hair.

Her fingers moved through the girl's hair with ease. Fatigue etched her brow. He knew she must be worn out from playing with all of them.

"I'm next," said the redhead.

"Then me," said another.

"Don't worry," Ivy tied a ponytail holder into the bottom of the girl's hair. "I'll do everyone's hair. Then we'll go in the living room and show Lauren's dad. I bet he'll even take a picture since you all look so pretty."

Carter opened the door wide. "You all do look pretty."

"Daddy," Lauren screamed and tried to cover her face and hair with her hands. "You have to wait till we're done."

Ivy lifted up her hand and mouthed the words *five more minutes*.

He nodded and raised his hands in surrender. "Okay. Okay. I'm out. When you're finished, I'll take your picture then we'll eat cake and ice cream and open presents."

"Yea!" the girls cheered in unison.

He walked back into the kitchen and pulled his camera out of the cabinet. By the time he made it back into the living room, the girls had started parading down the hall. Ivy already sat on the couch beside Clay. Gabe sat beside her, and Carter noted his lips seemed a bit glossier than normal. But at least there wasn't any color. The three cheered as each girl walked into the living room.

Once finished with their fashion walk, Carter motioned for them to get together. "Let's get a picture."

The girls giggled as they wrapped their arms around each other's necks and squeezed together. He took several shots then raised his hands. "Time for cake!"

"Yea!" They cheered again as they ran as a group into the kitchen with Clay and Gabe following at their heels.

Ivy extended her hand. "You sing and light candles and cut cake and put it on plates, and I'll take pictures."

He handed her the camera. "After all you've done, that sounds like a fair deal."

In a whirlwind, the girls ate, sang, and opened presents. By the time the last parent left, Ivy had flopped onto the couch with a sleeping Gabe on her chest. Carter smiled at her as he pointed to Clay. "Mind if I get him in bed before I take Gabe?"

"Don't worry. I ain't movin'."

Carter chuckled. "Spoken like a true teacher."

She grinned as she closed her eyes. Carter guided Clay into the bathroom to wash up and brush his teeth. After prayers, he tucked in his son then made his way back to the living room.

Ivy's body rested still against the cushion. Gabe nestled

up to her, thumb in mouth and his other hand wrapped around several strands of her hair. They both slept. It was one of the most beautiful sights he'd seen in a while, but he couldn't leave them that way. Couldn't bask in it. It hurt too much.

The camera still sat on the table beside her. Though he knew the photo would torture him, he couldn't help himself. He picked it up and snapped a shot of Ivy and Gabe. They looked happy and peaceful.

Clearing his throat, Carter touched Ivy's arm to wake her. Her eyelids fluttered open and she smiled up at him. His heart pounded with the urge to kiss her lips.

"I couldn't have done this without you."

"I was glad to help."

She was. The truth of it always shone on her face. Carter wanted to care about her. Yearned for it. But he didn't deserve it.

He leaned down to take Gabe from her arms. His mouth came just shy of her head. The scent of her shampoo tickled his senses. Unable to stop himself, he allowed a slight kiss to the top of her head before he stood with Gabe in his arms. He had to get out of there.

Chapter 13

The doorbell rang, and Ivy's eyelids fluttered open. The sun shone bright through blinds, and she forced herself to sit up in bed. Stretching her arms above her head, she allowed a long yawn.

"You look beautiful this morning, Sarah," Phil's deep voice boomed up the stairs and into her room. A soft smacking sound followed, and Ivy shuddered at what she knew had been a quick kiss.

"You don't look bad yourself," her mother's voice lilted upward. The last several weeks, her mother had been happier than Ivy had seen her in years. Having come to terms with her mom dating Phil, she now only warred with the jealous ache that she didn't have what Mom and Mirela had. "What's in the bag?"

"Fresh bagels, cream cheese, and French vanilla coffee for you and your girl. Where is Ivy?"

"The sleepyhead still hasn't gotten up."

Ivy forced her legs over the bed. Glancing at the clock, she realized she'd slept a good two hours later than usual for a Saturday morning. She'd promised Lauren she'd attend her game today, and now she only had an hour to get ready.

Throwing a sweatshirt over her T-shirt, she looked down at her pajama bottoms. She wouldn't go to town in the getup, but she supposed it was decent enough to eat breakfast with Phil and Mom. She padded down the stairs and into the kitchen. "Morning."

Phil grinned, and Ivy noted his salt-and-pepper hair was in need of a trim. White stubbles covered his chin and neck. No doubt it was his day off. And she couldn't deny the guy had definitely grown on her. He pointed to the counter. "Got some breakfast for you."

"Thanks." Ivy selected a blueberry bagel and regular cream cheese. She poured a cup of the flavored coffee in her favorite oversized mug. "So, what are you two doing today?"

"Shopping then lunch with my crew. You're more than welcome to join us," said Phil.

"Thanks for the offer, but I can't."

Her mother's cheeks blossomed red and Ivy wondered what they were shopping for. Surely not anything serious. Or expensive. They'd dated less than two months. Sure, they seemed to spend every spare moment together, but that didn't mean they were ready for something more permanent. Pushing the thought away, Ivy sat at the table across from them. Her mom took a sip of her coffee then put down the mug. "So, what are your plans today? I assumed you'd go with us to lunch."

Ivy bit back a growl. Her mother often assumed things for Ivy without asking. One of the reasons she'd debated moving out. She feared it would hurt her mom, but she needed to be treated as an adult.

"Going to Lauren's game then I thought I'd go for a hike." She looked out the window, already longing for the warm sun's kiss on her cheeks. She needed time to think, to pray, and meditate. She'd fretted over Carter and his children the past few months. Time alone with God would refresh and remind her that He was her first love.

Glancing back at her mother, she realized the woman bit her bottom lip. Her face contorted into a mixture of concern and frustration. Phil cupped his hand over her mom's, and Ivy turned her attention to him. "Sounds like a terrific plan," he said.

Ivy bit back a chuckle. Phil had been terrific, not only for her mother's happiness but to get Mom off Ivy's back. She popped the last bite of bagel into her mouth then wiped her hands on a napkin. "Thanks for breakfast, Phil. Gotta get ready. You two have fun."

She stood and pushed the chair under the table. Throwing away her trash, she heard her mother's muffled complaints that Ivy had no business spending time with a single father. She couldn't make out Phil's response, but she heard her mother's sigh. "You're right," her mom whispered. "She has to make her own choices."

Ivy made her way upstairs and into the bathroom. *God, thank You for Phil. If nothing else, he is getting Mom to stop trying to arrange my life.* After a quick shower, she dressed in a running outfit and tennis shoes and pulled her hair up in a ponytail. Not bothering to put on any makeup, she stared at her reflection. *Definitely not going for any beauty pageant awards today.*

She could have dolled up a bit more since she knew Carter would be at the game. But she never knew how he would respond to her. When he let go of his pride and guilt, he was kind and nice to be around. Other times, he was to the point or matter-of-fact or he avoided her altogether.

She grabbed her purse off the nightstand. *Which is why I need to spend a little extra one-on-one time with You today, Lord.*

When she walked downstairs, her mother and Phil had already gone. She locked the door, headed to the car, then drove to the school. The parking lot was packed with vehicles, and Ivy had to park on the side of the road.

She tapped the top of the steering wheel, unsure if she should try to sit with Carter and the boys or if she should sit by herself. If she sat with them, should she just walk up to them and plop down or wait until they invited her to join them? Rolling her eyes at her inner turmoil, she got out of the car and walked inside the gymnasium.

The gymnasium was packed nearly to capacity. She hadn't realized how many people attended recreational basketball games. Each kid's entire family—extended and all—must show up to watch their star. Skimming the audience, she didn't spy Carter and the boys.

Lauren saw her from the other side of the gym. She waved then grasped her short skirt with both hands and twisted side to side to show off her outfit. Ivy gave her a thumbs-up as she walked closer to the child.

"Miss Adams, we're up here."

Ivy looked toward the sound and spied Clay waving one hand and pointing to an empty seat beside him. Carter smiled at her. He didn't seem thrilled, but she didn't think he'd avoid her either. *At least not today. Tomorrow could be a different story.*

Since Lauren stood on the end closest to the bleachers, Ivy gave her a quick hug, only to be clobbered by another girl in her class as well as a student from the year before. She patted their backs. "Do good. I'm excited to watch you all."

Ivy made her way up the stairs, waving at any of the parents she recognized as she went. She pointed beside Clay. "Is this seat for me?"

He nodded with such enthusiasm she feared his neck would snap. Gabe wiggled away from his dad and meandered toward her. She lifted him onto her lap. "You like watching your sister cheer?"

"Uh-huh." Gabe clapped his hands. "Sissy does good."

Ivy glanced over Clay's head at Carter. "Hey."

He nodded. "How are you today, Ivy?"

"I'm good. You?"

"Good."

Ivy looked down at the court then over at Lauren. The child beamed as she punched out a cheer then kicked up one leg when her team scored.

Gabe played with the zipper on her jacket and Ivy glanced down at her running suit. Suddenly feeling self-conscious in her casual attire and makeup-free face in front of so many of her students and their parents, she pulled at the bottom of the jacket. Carter probably thought she looked like a ragamuffin.

Carter had never seen Ivy look more adorable. He knew she was a pretty woman. God had given him good vision enough to know a beauty when he saw one. But she was just as gorgeous when she wasn't all fixed up in her teacher outfits.

His reasons for not wanting to spend time with her had faltered over the past few days. He didn't normally watch television preachers, but he'd happened upon one while flipping channels in bed after Ivy left the birthday party. The man talked about guilt and how it festered like an open wound, and that when we picked at it, the wound grew until it became infected. And not just any infection, but one like MRSA, that could hurt others around you. People you loved.

He'd thought of Lauren, Clay, and Gabe and how much they loved Ivy. How she'd been a good influence in their lives. He hadn't pushed past his guilt for Mary's death, but he no longer wanted to avoid Ivy either. He'd do anything for his children. Including spend time with a woman who made him feel like a teenage boy with his first crush—weak in the knees and wet behind the ears.

Carter watched Lauren as she did a cartwheel on the sideline. She'd been happier the last few weeks. Had even invited a couple of friends over to spend the night. She'd acted more like a little girl and less like a miniature adult. Her brothers didn't get on her nerves as often, either.

Part of that may have been because Carter wasn't as burdened over money as he had been a few months ago. He'd landed two additional large jobs and was able to re-hire every worker who hadn't found other employment.

He also knew his daughter saw Ivy as a mother figure of sorts. The picture she'd drawn for Ivy was proof of it. If Mary were alive, Lauren wouldn't have felt such a gaping hole in her life. But Mary wasn't alive, and his daughter needed Ivy.

The game ended, and Lauren and the other cheerleaders raced to the center of the floor to join the basketball team in shaking hands with the opposing team.

Clay tugged on Ivy's arm sleeve. "We're going on a picnic. You wanna go?"

"Well, I…"

Carter turned toward her. "Actually, it's a modified picnic. We're going to pick up deli sandwiches and then take them to the park to eat in the pavilion." He shrugged. "Then I'll let the kids play a bit."

Gabe climbed around in her lap until he cupped her cheeks in his hands. "You push me?"

Lauren weeded her way through the families trying to make their way down the steps. "Miss Adams, you wanna go on a picnic with us?"

Gabe still smashed her cheeks with his chubby hands when she looked up at him. Carter couldn't hold back his chuckle. "You're more than welcome to come."

Ivy lifted Gabe's hands away from her face then acted as if she was going to gobble his belly. Gabe cackled and bent over. Ivy rearranged him in her lap then popped Lauren's nose with her index finger. "Of course I'll go."

Having decided to bring Ivy back to pick up her car, Carter buckled in the kids in the van then hopped in the driver's seat beside Ivy. He gripped the steering wheel until his knuckles turned white. Mary had been the last woman to sit in that spot.

Trying not to think about it, he focused on driving, ordering sandwiches, and then making it to the park. The kids chattered and asked Ivy questions, allowing him to work through his emotions in his mind and heart.

Once at the park, Ivy helped him get the kids' lunches together on the picnic table. She squirted hand sanitizer on each of their hands. She looked at him, bottle turned upside down. She nodded toward his hands, and he wrinkled his nose. "I hate the smell of that stuff."

"Are you allergic to it?"

"No."

"Then, I'm not letting you eat without cleaning your hands."

Carter laughed as he opened his palms, and she squirted a glob on his hands. "Yes, ma'am."

He sat across from her at the picnic table. Lauren and Clay sat on either side of her, while Gabe sat beside him. Clay started to take a bite of his sandwich, and Carter shook his head. "Let's say prayer first."

They bowed their heads, and Carter cleared his throat. "Lord, thank You for this food and for this beautiful day to spend at the park. Thank You that Lauren was such a great cheerleader today." He paused at the next words that almost slipped from his lips. He continued on, deciding to say them anyway. "Thank You that Ivy came with us."

He heard her slight gasp and hoped she wouldn't think he meant more than he did. Still, he continued, "She's been a blessing to my children."

Looking up, he gazed into her eyes. Sadness permeated from them, reminding him of the pitiful look his childhood dog had given each time they left him alone. Why would his prayer have hurt her feelings? He'd said he was thankful for her, and he was.

"I'm done. Can I go play?"

Carter looked at Clay. His cheeks bulged from a couple of bites of his sandwich. Before he could respond, Ivy pointed at his lunch. "You need to eat more."

Clay took two more bites. "How 'bout now?"

Carter shook his head.

Ivy tore his sandwich and pointed to the bigger half. "Eat that much."

Carter blinked, remembering Mary doing the same thing to Lauren when she tried to rush through a meal. He took a bite of his own sandwich and forced himself to chew it up.

"All done. Go play."

Carter looked at Gabe's food. His bottomless pit had swiped the wrapper clean. Not a crumb left. "Let's wait for sissy and brother."

Lauren and Clay finished, and Carter walked with Ivy and Gabe to the swings. Lauren jumped up on one and pumped her legs back and forth, while Carter pushed Clay and Ivy pushed Gabe.

Ivy had been quiet since he'd said the prayer, and he still didn't know what he'd done to upset her. He pushed Clay a little higher, the silence between them niggling at his gut. "You haven't told me much about your family."

"You met my mom. I think I already told you my dad passed away. I also have a sister who is my age." She lifted her hands. "Not twins. She was adopted."

"Really? Are you close?"

"Very close. She got married last year, and I don't see her as much."

"I'm sorry."

Carter watched as she bent down and resituated Gabe on the swing. The wind whipped her ponytail forward, and she had to pull strands away from her lips.

"My mom's dating now, too, which has been kind of weird."

Thankful her words distracted him, Carter blinked and looked away from her lips. "Yeah? How so?"

"Well, she and my dad were married twenty years. They were so close. Probably more so than most couples because they were missionaries and really had to depend on each other. Like I said, it's weird seeing her fall for another guy."

"I bet."

"Mirela says I need to think of it this way. Mom loved Dad. She'll always love Dad, but God has given her someone else to love as well." She released Gabe's swing, opened her palms upward and moved them up and down like a teeter-totter. "That it's not a love one or the other kind of thing, but like loving both."

She stopped and balanced her hands equally on both

side then looked at him. Her mouth fell open and pink washed down her cheeks and neck. "I'm sorry." Pulling her cell phone out of her jacket pocket, she said, "When did you say we were going back? I need to…I've got some things I need to do."

Carter nodded. "I'll take the kids down the slide. We'll leave in about ten minutes."

He walked away, her words clawing at his heart, threatening to break down his resolve for a life forever committed to Mary. He pushed them away. Didn't want to think about what she'd said and if it made sense.

Clay climbed up the steps and Carter helped Gabe follow his brother. He held Gabe's hand while the boy slid down the slide squealing with delight. Walking back to the steps, he noticed Ivy sitting on a swing, her gaze focused on the ground.

He knew she hadn't meant for the spiel to be directed at him, but they both knew it had been. However, unlike her mother, he didn't have any more love to give.

Chapter 14

Despite exhaustion, Ivy pushed herself higher up the mountain. Her knees wobbled and her chest burned, but embarrassment encouraged her on. She couldn't believe she'd said those things to Carter. He must think she was throwing herself at him, begging him to feel for her the way she felt for him.

Her cheeks flamed as she continued her trek. She'd passed her usual meditation spot. Couldn't risk being seen by anyone. She needed to be alone with God and her thoughts. Needed to be able to cry, really cry, out to Him.

Her hands trembled and she reached into her backpack and pulled out a bottle of water. Popping the top, she took a long gulp then continued her hike.

Sweat beaded on her forehead and she swiped it away with the back of her hand. Her chest burned and her throat felt drier than a day of lecturing without breaks. Spying a patch of rocks a few feet ahead, she pushed on. She hadn't passed any hikers in several minutes. She'd rest there.

Dropping to her bottom, she stretched out her legs and curled her toes toward her. She placed her hands on the rock behind her and stretched her back. Only a few times had she made it this high on the mountain. Normally, she and Mirela opted for a walk-halfway-up-then-sit-and-soak-in-God's-creation kind of hike. Today, she'd needed to push herself further.

Leaning forward, she bent her knees and rested her elbows on top of them. "God, I can't believe I said all that to Carter."

Her gaze swept the rolling hills and valleys below her. Some of the leaves had started to change to yellows, oranges, even a few reds. The sounds of nature surrounded her as her breathing and her mind settled. Crickets chirped and birds twittered and sang. She closed her eyes and breathed in God's masterpiece. No matter what her day was like, God was still amazing.

She opened her arms and lifted them to the heavens. No one was here to see her. Only she and her Sustainer. "God, You are always amazing."

Her heart flooded with thanksgiving for the opportunity to talk to her heavenly Father. Unlike the Israelites and all the people before Christ's death and resurrection, Ivy could step into the Holy of Holies and commune with her Lord and Savior. The humbling truth of it set her heart to pounding.

She opened her eyes. "Lord, if You are more beautiful than all this," she swiped her hands across the expanse, "then I can't imagine trying to look at the glory of Your face. Like Isaiah, I would fall to my knees, proclaiming my unclean lips."

Touching her hand to her mouth, she thought again of

what she'd said to Carter. "God, I feel like I love him. I adore the children. They are exhausting, just as Mirela said. And day in and day out would be harder than I know. I understand I truly don't know what it is to be a mother. I've never been one, but I love them, Lord. I do."

She curled her legs into a pretzel and pulled blades of grass off the ground. Twirling them in her fingers, she looked up at the heavens. "But I don't want him to think I was hinting that he should love me. I didn't mean for that to happen today."

She tossed the blades onto the ground. "Am I just infatuated with him? Do I simply think I love him because Mirela and Mom have found love? I am jealous of what they have. I admit openly to You that I want it, too."

Stretching her neck left and then right, she sighed at the quandaries of her own heart. She was a perfectionist. Known for overthinking things. Which was why she had to cling so tight to her Father.

She opened her Bible to Joshua, the place she'd left off in her daily reading through the Bible. Grinning, she'd read these passages many times before, especially during her years in college.

"'Be strong and courageous,'" she said the words aloud. She and Mirela had quoted the scripture to each other several times during finals week or over a particularly difficult paper that had to be written.

The scripture had been applicable to her life five years ago. She knew God would use it again now. Reading through the first chapter of Joshua, she opened her heart and mind to hear God's will for her life.

Her gaze lingered on the words, *Do not be afraid; do not be discouraged, for the Lord your God will be with you wherever you go.* She repeated the words aloud.

"God, I know You are with me wherever I go. I've

known that since I was a small girl. But where do You want me to go?"

She continued reading about the Israelites going into the Promised Land. They were stepping into a new life, fighting real battles, experiencing things they'd never known. And God told them to be strong and courageous. To have faith in Him.

Her heart filled with peace. She believed God had placed Carter and the children in her life for a purpose. To love them.

She would have to wait for Carter as he battled his guilt and pride, but she would step out in faith. She would trust God that He would work all things for good. Because she loved Him. She was called upon for His purpose. And until God showed her otherwise, she would love Carter and his children. She would help them when they needed it. She would pray for them throughout the day. And she would have faith in her Lord and Savior.

Joy overwhelmed her that God never ceased to use His Word to show her His ways for her life. She could call on Him in times of joy or despair—even confusion.

She stood to her feet and put the backpack over her shoulders. Gazing one last time at the beauty of God's creation, she praised Him once again that she could talk with Him.

Walking back down the mountain at a slower pace, she hummed one of her favorite contemporary Christian songs. She knew it wasn't going to be easy every moment, but being surrendered to God would help. She couldn't wait to see Carter and the kids again.

The past few days had been torture for Carter. Ivy's words at the park replayed in his mind like a scratched

DVD movie. He couldn't seem to move forward from that moment.

The kids were on fall break from school that week, which helped. Lauren's practices had been cancelled, and though he and her brothers endured hours of practices run by Lauren at home, Carter hadn't had to endure seeing Ivy at practices in the cafeteria.

But he'd missed her, and Gabe and Clay had asked more than once when she could come over for a visit. Lauren wanted her to fix her makeup again. The kids loved her, and he couldn't blame them. She was easy to get attached to.

He wiped his forehead with his arm. The dip in temperature had been nice, but he and his team had put in a rough morning at their jobsite. He'd known the day would be a tough one with a lot of physical labor, so he'd given his guys an extra fifteen minutes for lunch.

He needed the time to drop off the groceries he and the kids had purchased for the pantry. Donating had become a monthly habit for his family since they'd received groceries in their time of need. It was something they all participated in and enjoyed.

Walking into the fast-food restaurant, he wondered if Ivy worked at the pantry during fall break. Soon enough, he would find out. He ordered his lunch and picked up his tray to find a place to sit.

"Carter."

He scanned the room for who had called his name when he spied his pastor motioning him. Carter made his way toward Bill. It had been a while since the two of them had talked outside of church, mainly because Carter was always busy with the kids. He liked talking with his pastor. Only a few years older than him, he and Bill shared many of the same likes in sports and outdoor activities.

Carter sat across from him. "Hey, Bill. How's it going?"

Bill nodded. "Good. I just left the hospital. Was visiting Sam after his surgery. He's doing well."

"That's good to hear." Carter had forgotten about his friend's kidney stone surgery. A few years ago, Carter would have tried to visit Sam. Mary would have probably made them dinner or a dessert of some kind. Since her death, he barely kept up with his own house let alone what was happening with his friends.

Carter bowed his head for a quick prayer then took a long swallow of his soft drink. He and Sam had even completed several Bible studies together.

"What's wrong, Carter?"

"Nothing. Just feeling guilty that I'd forgotten about Sam's surgery."

"You're a busy guy. Honestly, I don't know how you do it. I wouldn't know how to survive without Cindy."

Carter shrugged "You do what you gotta do."

The statement was true, but it didn't make the task any easier. He missed Mary for more reasons than he would have ever fathomed two years ago. Their teamwork allowed both of them to attend Bible studies and spend time with friends. Things they enjoyed apart from each other. Not only had he lost the times they spent together, but he'd lost time with his friends as well.

"Cindy said Lauren's teacher takes her to cheerleading practice."

Carter had forgotten that Bill's second daughter was on the cheerleading squad that shared the cafeteria with Lauren's team. "Yep. She's been a lot of help. The kids love her."

Bill raised his eyebrows and ducked his chin. "Is that all? Seems mighty nice of her to take Lauren to practice twice a week."

Carter frowned. "Yes. That's all." He took a bite of his hamburger and swallowed it down without chewing all the way.

Bill sat back in his chair. "Still struggling with guilt, I see. I was afraid of that."

"Look. I know you're the pastor and it's your job to be in tune with the Lord all the time..."

"It's your job every bit as much as it's mine."

Carter didn't respond. He chewed on Bill's words, knowing they were true. He exhaled a breath. "Sorry I snapped at you. I guess I am still feeling guilty." He touched his chest. "Because I am guilty."

"Of what? Forgetting the formula? Do you know how many items over the years Cindy has called me to bring home that I have forgotten? More than she or I could even begin to count."

Carter tried not to laugh. Bill was known for his forgetfulness. The church's secretary spent as much time making sure he was where he was supposed to be as she did anything else in the office.

Bill swatted the air with one hand. "You're forgiven already. It's done. You can't change it. And you're allowing the enemy to use guilt as a tool to keep you from a full relationship with God. And possibly someone else."

Shocked by Bill's frustration with him, Carter didn't know how to respond. Was God quiet with him because he wouldn't release the guilt?

Bill looked at his watch. "Oops. I don't want to leave on that note, but I'm already five minutes late for an appointment." He stood and picked up his tray. Patting Carter on the shoulder, he said, "I care about you, Carter. I don't doubt your love for the Lord, your children, or Mary, but it's time to put the guilt aside and move forward."

Carter didn't speak as Bill walked out of the restaurant. He didn't know what to say. Surely, he hadn't allowed Satan a foothold into his life. A quote he'd heard somewhere traipsed through his mind. *God is never the author of shame.*

His brain tried to replay his pastor's words and Ivy's words at the park. It was all too much for him. He finished his burger and took a few more drinks before he threw away the trash.

He needed some time alone with God and His Word. Though he struggled with the notion, he would try to allow whatever God had to say to penetrate his heart. No matter what, he would make time tonight.

Hopping in the van, he drove to the pantry. Ivy's car was parked a few places away from him. Sucking in a deep breath, he grabbed several bags out of the backseat. He pushed open the pantry door and waited for her to greet him.

Brent walked out of the office, and Carter's heart dropped. His expression must have shown his disappointment because Brent scowled. He jutted his thumb behind him. "She's in the back. You want me to go get her?"

Carter shook his head, wondering about the aggravation in Brent's tone. He knew the man liked Ivy. Had she told him she didn't feel the same way? It was selfish of Carter, but he couldn't help hoping it was true. "No. I'll just leave these groceries. I've got some more in the van."

"Need some help?"

"No. I got it."

Carter went to his vehicle and scooped the rest of the bags out of the backseat. He went back into the pantry, and his heart dropped again. This time because Ivy stood in front of him.

Just like Saturday, she wore a running suit, no makeup, and her hair in a ponytail. Again, she took his breath away, and he was glad his hands were full of groceries or he might have swept her into his arms.

"Hi." She blushed at the single word, and Carter's chest tightened.

"Hey. I've…" He placed the bags on the ground. "The kids have missed you."

"I've missed them, too. In fact…" She clasped her hands together and shifted her weight from one foot to the other. "I wondered if I could come get them and take them for ice cream or something. You could come, too."

"The kids would love that." He would love it, too. Then he remembered his promise to spend time in God's Word tonight. It had to be more than coincidence that he'd made that promise and then God provided a way for him to do it. "I would like to go with y'all, but I have something I need to do tonight."

She looked down at the ground, and he could tell she was disappointed. Seeming to rally her will, she looked back up at him. "That's okay. I'll still come get the kids. Seven o'clock okay?"

"Sounds great. I'll let you surprise them."

She nodded, and he waved as he walked back to the van. *God, use that time to show Yourself to me. I can't handle this roller coaster I'm riding each time I see her. You know I've never been one for amusement parks.*

Chapter 15

Ivy knocked on the front door to Carter's house. Lauren opened it. She squealed and wrapped her arms around Ivy's waist. "Miss Adams!"

"What? Who is it?" Clay peeked around the door and cheered when he saw her. He hugged her side. Gabe rounded the door and wrapped himself around her leg.

She laughed. "I've missed you, too, but I can't move."

Carter pulled them one after another off her. "Go get your shoes on. Miss Adams is taking you for ice cream."

Lauren's eyes widened. "Really?"

"Really." Ivy patted the girl's head. They scampered down the hall, and Ivy added, "You need a jacket, also."

Carter raised his eyebrows. "Told you they missed you."

Haven't you missed me, too? I've fallen asleep and awakened thinking about you, Carter. She wanted to shake some sense into him. Or more accurately, shake some love.

He held out his keys. "I thought it might be easier for

you to drive my van, so we wouldn't have to switch Gabe's car seat."

"Oh. Okay." Ivy took the keys. She was surprised at how excited he seemed for her to leave. It hadn't been too long ago that he'd acted as if she might kidnap his children given time alone with them.

The kids raced into the living room with shoes and jackets on. Clay's hung off his shoulder, and Ivy bent down and fixed it. "Looks like we're ready."

A moment of anxiety washed over her. She'd babysat plenty of times as a teenager. She taught a classroom of twenty-six seven-year-olds. She'd even taken care of Bella and Benny by herself on several occasions. But she'd never done an outing alone.

Carter clapped his hands. "Well, you have my cell number if you need anything. Why don't you give me your car keys, just in case?"

"Uh, okay." She fished her keys out of her purse and handed them to Carter.

"You want some help getting them into their seats?"

"I can buckle Gabe, Daddy," said Lauren.

"Great. Then you're set." Carter bent down and hugged and kissed each child on the forehead. "Be good for Miss Adams."

The children ran out the door, and Ivy waved at Carter then followed them. Her hands trembled when she slipped into the driver's seat and familiarized herself with the gears, lights, and heater.

"We're all buckled," Lauren announced.

Ivy turned around and saw that all of them had their seat belts on. She blew out a breath. She was worrying for nothing. They were great kids. She'd never had a moment's trouble with them. Pulling out of the driveway, she headed to the frozen yogurt place.

Once inside, she squirted hand sanitizer on each of their hands then helped them put frozen yogurt in their cups. She pointed to the various condiments—fruit, chocolates, nuts, gummies, and more. "You can pick three different kinds to put in your cup. Tell me which ones you want, and I'll help you."

She lifted Gabe onto her hip. He pointed to the gummies and she shook her head. "You're too little for them."

"No. Gabe can have gummy," he said, pointing at his chest.

"Dad lets him have one at a time. He watches him chew them up," said Lauren. She reached for the chocolate chips and Ivy helped her spoon them in the cup without spilling.

Ivy patted Gabe's chest. "Okay. I'll let you have some gummies, but just a few. You have to eat them one at a time."

Gabe nodded. "Chew them all up."

"That's right."

Sprinkles spilled to the floor beside her, and Ivy looked to see Clay's shirt button had gotten stuck on the canister and pulled it out of place. Clay puckered his lower lip. "I'm sorry."

"It's okay." Ivy bent to pick up the canister and Gabe dropped his cup of yogurt down her leg.

"Uh-oh," Gabe said.

Ivy gasped and stood to her full height. She grabbed napkins off the counter and tried to wipe the yogurt from her jeans.

"Here. Let me help you, ma'am." Sounding perturbed, one of the workers, a girl who probably attended the local community college, took the now-empty cup from Gabe's hand. He screamed, and the girl grabbed a new cup and put it in his hand.

Trying not to think about the sticky substance seeping

through her jeans, Ivy smiled at the girl. "I'll get him some more yogurt, if you don't mind helping with the sprinkles."

She turned and saw Clay scooping sprinkles off the floor and sticking them in his mouth. "Clay, no!"

He stood and his lower lip quivered. Ivy pushed away thoughts of the many germs that most likely dwelled on the shop's concrete floor. The worker grabbed a broom from the back of the building and swept up. Tears welled in Clay's eyes. "I wanted sprinkles."

"We don't have anymore, kid," the teen snapped, and Ivy bit her tongue to keep from laying in to the girl. He hadn't meant to spill the condiment. And Ivy hadn't meant to scare the life out of him either.

"I'll help him, Miss Adams." Lauren placed her cup on the counter beside the register, and took Clay's hand. "Which other ones you want?"

Ivy made her way back to the yogurt and lifted the handle to the vanilla flavor and poured more for Gabe. By the time she'd filled his cup with a few gummies and chocolate chips, Lauren and Clay stood by the register waiting for her to pay for their dessert.

"You want me to wait for you to get one for yourself?" asked the cashier.

Ivy looked at the frozen yogurt. Her favorite fall flavor seemed to call her name. She'd planned to get some. The frozen yogurt place had been one of her favorite hangout spots through high school and college. Lots of fun memories, and she still loved the desserts.

Gabe tried to jump out of her arms to reach his cup. She decided it wouldn't be wise to try to eat her own treat while trying to keep him from choking on a gummy. She shook her head. "No. I'm fine."

The cashier placed all three cups on the scale and weighed them. Ivy paid then grabbed Gabe's yogurt and walked to a circular table. The chairs were tall, and Clay had to climb up onto his. Too afraid for Gabe to sit by himself, she sat him in her lap.

She sniffed. Something smelled atrocious. She looked around her, wondering what the stench could have been. Realization struck her, and she frowned. *Surely not.* Pulling on the back of Gabe's pants, the smell assaulted her with gusto. "Did anyone happen to pick up Gabe's backpack?"

"No," said Lauren.

"Not me," said Clay. Ivy cringed when he licked his spoon all the way to the handle.

She placed her elbow on the table and rubbed her forehead. They couldn't take the frozen yogurt in the van, and she couldn't make them throw it away. They'd only just started eating it.

She had no choice but to allow Gabe to sit in his soiled diaper on her lap until they finished. Gabe waved his hand in front of his nose. "Gabe made a stinky."

"Yes, Gabe did."

A family walked by them, and the little boy pinched his nose as he looked up at his father. "Dad, did you toot?"

"No, son." The man placed his hand against the boy's back and nudged him toward the frozen yogurt.

Lauren started to giggle. Soon Clay joined her. Suddenly, the whole thing struck Ivy as funny and she chuckled as well. She pointed to their cups. "You all better hurry before they kick us out."

By the time they reached the house Ivy thought she would puke from Gabe's aroma. Carter opened the door and fanned his hand in front of his nose. Ivy wrinkled her nose. "Yeah. We forgot the backpack."

Carter's eyes lit up and he busted out in laughter. He waved them inside. "So, you had a good time?"

He took Gabe and walked back to the bedroom. Lauren and Clay followed, telling about the spilled sprinkles, the dumped frozen yogurt, and the boy's question to his father. Ivy stood inside the door, unsure what to do. She couldn't leave because she had to give him his keys and get hers.

Gabe ran back into the living room. "All clean."

Ivy rubbed his head. "Well, I'm glad, little man."

She looked up and swallowed. Carter stood just a few feet away from her. His eyes twinkled in merriment. "You had fun?"

"I did."

"You sure about that?" He glanced down at her jeans. She let her hand fall beside her leg as if she were advertising a new car. "I'm trying out the latest scent. It's called vanilla frozen yogurt."

Carter grinned. "I think they had fun."

"I really did, too."

Carter studied her, and Ivy bit her bottom lip. Unsure what to do with the silence, she held up his keys. He took them and grabbed hers off the end table.

"So, listen." She pressed the keys between her fingers. "My sister's family and my mom and Phil are going hiking this Saturday. Mirela's daughter, Bella, is Lauren's age, and I wondered if you all would like to come."

Carter's expression was unreadable. She wished she could sneak up inside his brain to know what he was thinking. She might even make a few adjustments regarding his pride-filled, guilty conscience while she was in there. He finally nodded. "I think that sounds like fun."

Carter had gotten lost after Phil introduced him to the second Jim in his family. One was his son, the other a son-in-law. At least Mirela and her family would be easy to remember since Ivy had shared so much about them. When

Ivy invited him to hike with her family, he hadn't realized it would include twenty or more people. By the look on her face when they'd pulled into the campsite at the base of the mountain, Ivy hadn't known it either.

He glanced back at Ivy and Sarah. It was obvious Sarah hadn't expected Ivy to bring him and the kids. And she didn't approve.

He couldn't say that he blamed the woman. If Lauren brought home a guy with three kids to boot he'd wonder if Lauren had made the best choice. But after chewing on Ivy's and Bill's words and soaking in some scripture, Carter determined to give it a try.

Not that Ivy had ever told him she cared about him as more than his kids' father. He couldn't say with certainty she would be willing to pursue a relationship. But he was. At least he wanted to try.

Phil patted his back. "I'm glad you and your kiddos came."

"We were glad for the invitation. Beautiful day. The kids will get some exercise."

Phil's eyes glassed over as he looked past Carter. "It's going to be the best of days."

Carter turned in the direction Phil looked and saw Sarah. She picked up his youngest grandchild, a three-month-old boy, and rocked him in her arms.

Ivy stomped toward him. Frustration wrapped her features, and she grabbed his hand in hers. "Let's catch up with my sister and her family. They've already headed up the hill."

She nodded to Phil, and Carter waved at him with his free hand. "See you in a bit."

Phil seemed to have already forgotten about Carter as he made his way to Sarah. The man was smitten. By the expression on Sarah's face when she saw him approaching, Carter knew Ivy's mother felt the same way.

Ivy whistled. "Come on, kids. Let's hike."

All three of his children hustled toward them, and Carter couldn't hold back a grin. No one else in the crew came running. Only his three.

She still held his hand, though they'd walked several yards from the picnic area. Carter didn't let go, deciding to relish the feel of her softness. Guilt at the pleasure he felt tried to wiggle its way into his mind. He shoved it aside. God wanted him to walk in freedom, to be willing to love again.

Clay walked up beside Ivy and placed his hand in her free one. Carter noticed she looked down at their intertwined hands. She gazed up at him, and he squeezed her hand, hoping she wouldn't let go. Her cheeks darkened and she glanced back at Clay but didn't release his hand. "Are you having fun?"

"Uh-huh."

Lauren shoved an earthworm toward him. "Look what I found."

Clay screamed, pressing closer to Ivy's leg. Carter doubled over in laughter. "Why don't you see if you can help her find some more?"

"I will." Gabe walked behind Lauren, trying to be sure he stepped in her exact footprints.

Though hesitant, Clay followed his brother and sister. Ivy let go of his hand, walked to Gabe, and zipped up his jacket.

Carter flexed his fingers. He wished for a reason to take her hand in his again. Making his way to her and the children, he stood beside her and watched the kids dig through the soft ground. It hadn't rained for a few days, but the damp air kept the ground from drying out. He turned to

Lauren. "It doesn't look like we're going to make it up the hill. I don't think we're going to leave this spot."

She settled onto a log. "That's okay. I enjoy watching the kids."

He knew that she meant it. She cared about his children as if they were her own. She didn't hesitate to correct them when they needed it, but more importantly, she showered them with love and affection.

An hour passed and they still hadn't moved. Ivy's sister and her family approached, and Ivy hopped up off the log. She wiped her hands on her jeans. "Looks like it's time to head back."

Mirela nudged her toddling boy forward. "Yeah. We're actually running a little late. Benny wanted to walk."

By the time they'd returned to the picnic area, Sarah and Phil had already grilled hot dogs and hamburgers on the stone fire pit. Bags of chips and containers of potato salad and coleslaw sat on one of the tables. Ivy pulled wet wipes out of her purse and started cleaning his kids' hands. She handed one to him, and he raised his eyebrows at her. She wrinkled her nose. "Don't even think about touching that food without wiping off your hands."

Carter bit back a laugh. Spoken like a true mother.

Phil lifted his hands to get everyone's attention. He wrapped his arm around Sarah's back. "Sarah and I are glad you were all able to meet us here for a hike and picnic. It's important to us that you get to know each other."

He looked down at Sarah, and Carter heard Ivy's gasp beside him.

Phil continued, "We know we haven't dated long, but Sarah and I aren't spring chickens. And when it's right, it's right."

He patted Sarah's back. "Show them your ring."

"No." Ivy murmured under her breath.

Sarah lifted her hand, and Phil's daughters raced to her to see the gem. Ivy stood and walked toward the woods.

Mirela nudged his elbow. "Go. She needs to talk to someone. I've got the kids."

"Thanks."

Carter followed Ivy. He had no idea what he would say to her, but he knew he could listen. He passed several trees before he spotted her with her back to him. Hearing her soft cry, he prayed, *God, give me the right words.*

He touched her shoulder, and she spun around and planted her face in his chest. An ache filled him as he wrapped his arms around her. It had been so long since he'd held the woman he loved.

He did love her. Despite his best efforts to torture himself, she'd been too hard to resist. He pulled her closer and raked his fingers through her hair.

"How could she just up and get engaged to him? She loved my father. I know she did."

Carter pulled her just far enough away from him to be able to look into her eyes. "She still loves your father. Only now she loves Phil as well. Remember you told me that."

He wanted to tell her that he felt the same about her. That he'd fallen madly in love with her. That she'd stolen his thoughts, awake and asleep.

She gazed up at him, and he allowed himself to drink in the beauty of her eyes, the color of the sky on a clear day. His gaze traveled to her lips, the perfect shade of pink, so full and slightly parted.

He couldn't take it anymore. Lowering his head, he captured her lips to his. Utilizing every ounce of strength, he pulled away from her. But it wouldn't do. He cupped her cheeks in his hands and drew her close again.

Her lips were soft, sweet, and it had been too long. Her touch felt right and yet hurt to his core. He pulled away from her again. For a moment, her eyes remained closed and her lips parted.

She opened her eyes and stared at him. "How can she already love him?"

The same way I love you. He wanted to scream the words at the top of his lungs. But she didn't want to hear that. He must have been wrong to think she had feelings for him. If she thought her mother wrong, she most certainly felt the same about him.

He touched her cheek. "Sometimes love happens when you aren't looking. But what you said the other day at the park, you were right. Your mother can love your father all the days of her life, but she can love Phil as well."

Turning away from her, he walked back to the picnic. He wished he could pack up the kids and take them home, but they were in the middle of eating and to do so would cause a fight, which would make him have to explain why he was leaving so soon.

He grabbed a paper plate off the table and filled it with food. Sarah came up beside him. "I'm afraid I haven't given you much of a chance. May we start over?" She extended her hand. "Hi. My name is Sarah. I'm Ivy's mother."

That was just great. Her mother wanted to make amends while Ivy had run miles away from him. Out of politeness, he shook her hand. "I'm Carter."

"Nice to meet you, Carter." She walked back to the table and sat beside Phil. They looked at each other like lovesick pups, and Carter wished again that he could take his kids and go.

On his way to his kids' table, he tapped Mirela's shoulder. "I think she'd rather talk to you than me."

Pity wrapped Mirela's features, and it was all Carter could do not to rip his plate in two. Making his way to the table, he forced himself to shove the food down his throat. Once his kids finished, he threw away their garbage.

He couldn't remember the guy's name, but he asked Mirela's husband if they could be sure Ivy made it back to her house. He needed to take the kids home.

Tuckered out from digging in the dirt, he was able to get them all in the van without much of a squabble. On the way home, he wallowed in the ache of his heart. *God, I can't believe I kissed her. She must think me a complete fool.*

He sighed as he turned into the driveway. The guilt hadn't hurt as bad as her not loving him.

Chapter 16

Ivy feigned sleep as she laid her head against the window of Phil's car. She felt like a teenager, riding in the backseat of the car. Mom and Dad in the front.

Only it wasn't her father driving the car.

She blew out a long breath, allowing her pity party to take hold of her heart. In a day's time, she'd gone from determined to conquer the world to begging God to get her to her bedroom so she could flop on the bed and sleep her troubles away.

Phil pulled into the driveway, and Ivy hopped out of the car. She couldn't stand the thought of hearing or seeing them kiss each other good-bye. Charging into the house, she ran up to her bedroom and shut the door.

The front door closed, and Ivy smashed her pillow over her head, praying her mom wouldn't decide she wanted to talk. Carter's kiss flooded her mind, sending a tingle to her toes. She wrinkled her nose. Why had he done that? She knew he still mourned his wife.

"Ivy Adams, you come down here right now."

Ivy sat up at the sound of Mirela's voice. She couldn't remember the last time she'd heard her softhearted sister yell. Still, she had no intention of talking to either one of them. "What do you want?"

"We need to hash this out right now," her sister yelled again. "Either you come down or we're coming up there."

Ivy rolled her eyes. The last thing she wanted was all three of them squished together on her bed. She forced herself up and walked down the stairs. Her mother already sat in the rocking chair. Mirela pointed to the couch. "Now sit."

Ivy looked around the room. "Where's Josif and the kids?"

"Josif took them to the park until we can work this out."

Guilt filled her. It was getting late, and they still had a forty-five-minute drive home. She knew the kids were getting tired. "You can call Josif. Mom and I will talk."

Mirela shook her head. "I'm staying until we're all happy."

Ivy bit the inside of her cheek. Then she'd better send her husband and the kids home. This could take a while.

"Is it Phil? Do you not like him?"

Her mother's voice was soft, and Ivy looked at her. She'd changed a great deal in the few months she'd known Phil. Backed off from trying to control Ivy's life. At least most of the time. Ivy shook her head. "No. I like him a lot."

"Then what is it?"

Ivy warred with the right words to say. She smacked her hands against her thighs. "It's the short time you've known him. It's Dad. It's Brent. It's a lot of things."

"I shouldn't have pushed you to like Brent."

"Yeah. Now it's really uncomfortable trying to work with him."

"I am sorry."

Ivy peeked at her mother, who looked at the ceiling while she rocked. Ivy had seen that look before. When they were about to be grounded for doing something wrong. When she wanted to get her point across. When they'd found out her father wasn't going to make it. Her mother pondered what to say and how to say it.

"When your dad died, I threw my whole life into you girls. I couldn't stand the thought of losing either of you. We all know I tried to keep Mirela from Josif."

Ivy looked at her sister, and they nodded at each other. Mirela wrinkled her nose. "Yes, I remember."

Her mother continued, "When she married him, I felt like you were all I had left. I realized I wanted you to have love as Mirela had, as your father and I had. And Brent seemed like such a perfect choice."

"But he wasn't, Mom."

"I know. I was wrong." Her mother clasped her hands. "And as far as Phil goes, I hadn't expected to meet him."

Ivy's heart constricted. She'd been the one who'd wanted to set them up.

"Ivy expected it," said Mirela.

Ivy scowled at her sister.

Her mother furrowed her brow. "What do you mean?"

Ivy let out a long breath. "The truth is I wanted you to start seeing Phil for therapy because I thought you'd be a good match. Then maybe you'd get off my back about Brent."

Her mother rocked forward and burst out laughing. "Are you serious? You were matchmaking? And now you're upset that it worked?"

"Sounds a little silly, doesn't it?" said Mirela.

Ivy glared at her sister. It did sound silly. Her feelings congealed in a jumbled mess, making her feel more like a sixteen-year-old instead of a grown woman.

"Then what is the problem?" asked her mom.

Ivy shrugged. "It just seems so fast, Mom."

"It has been fast, but I'm not young, and I want to enjoy the rest of my years with him. We share a love for the most important things in life—God, our families, and people."

"Everyone but Dad?"

Her mother got up and moved to the couch beside Ivy. "What about Dad? You know I loved your father. I still do. Phil loved his wife. Still does. We were both blessed with wonderful marriages—which is why we miss what we had."

She reached up and brushed a strand of Ivy's hair behind her ear. "I think this has more to do with Carter than it does me and Phil."

Ivy frowned and gawked at her mother. "What could this possibly have to do with Carter?"

"You love him, honey. It's plain as the nose on your face."

Ivy couldn't deny it. Didn't even try to. He'd kissed her today, but she hadn't put her finger on why since he'd made it clear so many times that it was the kids, not him, who wanted her around. "He still loves his wife."

Mirela sat forward in her chair and grabbed Ivy's hand. "That's not a bad thing. Shows he makes promises and keeps them."

"And I think he loves you, too."

Ivy looked at her mom. She wrapped her arm around Ivy's shoulder. "Ah, honey. I haven't been good about Carter. I didn't want to give him a chance because of his kids and his job. I'm embarrassed that I behaved that way."

Tears welled in Ivy's eyes. Mirela handed her a tissue

from her back pocket. Ivy giggled. Since her sister had become a mother, she was always ready with tissues, wipes, and the like.

Ivy turned toward her mom. "I do like Phil. And I am glad you're happy."

Her mother wrapped her arms around her. "I love you, Ivy."

Mirela hopped up and wrapped her arms around both of them. "Yay. We're all better."

She let go and pulled her cell phone out of her pocket.

Ivy wiped her eyes. "Mirela, what are you doing?"

She lifted her index finger to quiet Ivy. "Come on back, Josif. All is right in the world again."

Ivy and her mother laughed at Mirela's dramatics.

Mirela pointed her finger at both of them. "Hey. The two of you can just change into some comfy clothes and head to bed. Not me. Bedtime is an hour or longer process."

Ivy pulled her sister into another hug. "Thanks for staying, Mirela."

Her sister whispered, "Before long you're going to understand exactly what I mean."

Carter leaned Gabe back in the tub to rinse the shampoo out of his hair. A scream sounded from the living room, and Carter yanked his youngest out of the tub and wrapped the towel around him.

Lauren ran into the bathroom, her eyes big as three-inch dowel rods. "Daddy, hurry!"

Clay's wails filled the house, as Carter ran with his towel-covered child into the living room. He gasped when he saw Clay lying on the floor behind the couch. He held his arm, and Carter could tell by the bump on the lower half that he had broken it.

He put Gabe down and checked Clay's body to be sure

his arm was the only injury. He looked at Lauren. "What happened?"

Tears streamed down her cheeks. "We were jumping, and he fell and hit the end table, and…"

Clay continued to scream, and Carter waved at Lauren. "It's okay, sweetie. He'll be fine. Just go get Ms. Anna."

Lauren ran out of the house, and Carter lifted Clay and set him on the couch. Pain and fear etched his son's face. He patted Clay's head. "It's going to be okay. Let me get Gabe dressed. We'll go to the hospital to make it better."

Clay's bottom lip quivered. He cried as Carter raced into Gabe's room and grabbed clothes to put on his youngest son.

Lauren raced back into the house. Her whole body trembled, and Carter knew she was afraid for her brother. "She's not home, Daddy."

He gave her a quick hug. "It's okay. You wanna call Miss Adams for me?"

She nodded, and he handed her the cell phone from his front pocket. He dressed Gabe then went back to the living room with Clay.

"He fell off the couch."

Carter could hear Lauren's words from the other room. Grabbing Clay's shoes from beside the front door, he put them on him then put on his own.

"She said she'd meet us at the hospital, Daddy."

Carter nodded. Good thinking. They wouldn't have to wait. He turned toward Lauren and Gabe. "Go get in the van and buckle up. I'm going to carry Clay."

"I'm scared." Clay's voice quivered as he continued to cry.

Carter kissed the child's forehead, dampened from sweat. "It'll be okay. You'll see."

Once at the hospital, he signed in and they sat in the

lobby. He didn't see Ivy. He hoped she'd arrive soon. It would be hard to take all three of them back to the examining room. He sat Clay on his lap and rubbed his son's hair and cheek to keep him calm.

The automatic doors opened and Ivy ran in. She scanned the room, her eyes alight with concern and fear.

"Miss Adams!" Lauren hopped off the seat beside Carter. She wrapped her arms around Ivy's legs as sobs overtook her.

Carter's chest tightened. Lauren had been helpful and tried to be strong the entire trip over in spite of being scared.

Ivy kept her hand on Lauren's back as she walked toward them. Without a second thought, she scooped Gabe into her lap and sat beside him and Clay. She touched Clay's back, and his son offered her a pitiful look. "Oh honey, I'm so sorry."

A nurse opened the door leading to the emergency room and called, "Clay Smith."

Carter locked gazes with Ivy. "You got here just in time."

"Don't worry about Lauren and Gabe. I've got them." She nestled both of them closer to her. She touched Clay's chin. "You'll be okay, buddy."

He nodded even though his lower lip still quivered. Carter stood and carried his son to follow the woman.

"So, what brings you in?"

"He fell off the couch. His arm is broken."

They walked into an examining room and the woman motioned for Carter to place Clay on the bed, but Clay wouldn't let go. She smiled and pointed to the chair. "It's okay."

Carter sat and maneuvered Clay around so the woman

could see his arm. She pursed her lips. "Looks like Dad is right. We'll get some X-rays, but I believe it is broken."

She turned away from them and opened a drawer. Handing Clay an unwrapped sucker, she said, "Tell me again, hon, how it happened?"

Clay took the candy with his free hand. "Lauren and I were jumping on the couch, and I tried to show her my flip off the back."

He looked up at Carter, realizing he was tattling on himself for something he wasn't supposed to do. He ducked his head. "And my arm hit the table."

"Which is why we're not supposed to jump on the couch," Carter added.

The nurse patted Clay's head. "Happens all the time." She pinched his nose. "But you better listen to your daddy next time."

Minutes dragged by as they waited to go back for X-rays then waited for the X-rays to be read, and then waited some more for the doctor to share the results. Carter pulled out his phone to text Ivy to be sure they were okay, but he couldn't get a signal.

More than an hour had passed and he knew Gabe was probably being difficult since it was past his bedtime. Clay had nestled himself against Carter's chest and fallen asleep.

He wished he could talk to Ivy. In only a few short months, she'd become like a mother to his children. They still wanted him when they were scared or injured, but she was their second pick. Even tonight, Lauren had felt comfortable to break down and show her emotions to Ivy.

He thought of his daughter. She'd changed this year. For the better. The bitterness and anger she'd felt since Mary's death had dissipated. She still got angry, still threw fits sometimes, but she'd started playing again. She laughed.

She enjoyed spending time with friends and even her brothers. Ivy had been the reason for all that.

He loved her. Everything about her. She was beautiful inside and out. He didn't even mind her insistence about the hand sanitizer. He wanted her to love him in return.

Disbelief still settled on him that he'd kissed her today. So much had happened. It seemed to have been eons ago since he'd felt her lips against his. She'd been so upset about her mom. Hadn't pulled away from him, but she hadn't given herself to the kiss either.

Still, her lips felt wonderful. Tantalizing. Feelings he'd put away years before stirred inside him. A kiss wasn't enough. He wanted Ivy as his wife, as the mother of his children.

Carter bit back a groan. But she had to love him. Not just the kids. He'd had seven amazing years of marriage with Mary. He wouldn't, couldn't settle for anything less.

"So, how are we doing in here?"

Carter jumped and broke away from his thoughts at the doctor's voice.

"Sorry 'bout that. Didn't mean to sneak up on you."

Clay didn't wake, so Carter finagled his hand free and shook the white-haired man's hand. "It's okay. So, what are we doing?"

The man sat down on the swivel chair. "Well, his arm is definitely broken, but it's a clean break. I'll set it tonight, but because of swelling, I'll have to put him in a sling for a few days. Then, we'll get him in a cast."

Carter nodded. He assumed as much, but he dreaded waking up Clay so they could set his arm. He remembered breaking his leg as a boy. It wasn't an enjoyable ordeal.

The doctor scrunched his face. "You ready to wake him up?"

"Don't have a choice, do we?"

He shook his head, and Carter jostled Clay awake. By the time this night was over, Carter would need a little comfort of his own. He wished he could get it from the blond in the other room.

Chapter 17

Ivy paced the floor of the emergency room lobby while Gabe and Lauren colored a picture. Thankful she'd had the good sense to grab some snacks, games, crayons, and coloring books, she couldn't believe they'd been waiting two full hours. The lobby had been practically empty the entire evening. Surely, Carter and Clay hadn't had to wait on the doctor.

Anxiety welled within her. Unless something was wrong and Clay needed surgery. She hadn't gotten a good look at his arm. Not that she'd know anything anyway. She certainly didn't have much experience with broken bones. A few of her students over the years had come to school with casts, but she hadn't seen them when the break actually happened.

She rubbed her hands together. She couldn't wait any longer. Walking up to the receptionist, she smiled at the middle-aged, dark-haired woman. She pointed back at

Gabe and Lauren. "We've been waiting a long time, and I wonder if we could go back and check on their brother?"

The woman snarled as she plopped her elbow on the desk and dropped her chin into her fist. Ivy blinked at the woman's grumpy disposition, hoping whoever was taking care of Clay was nicer. With her free hand, she pointed at Ivy with her pen. "You the mother?"

"No."

"The aunt, sister, cousin?"

"No. I'm a…" What would she call herself? She had to be more than a friend, though she'd love to be Carter's girlfriend. Or the kids' second mother. The woman lifted her eyebrows and cocked her head. Ivy sputtered. "I'm a friend."

The woman dismissed her. "Sorry, lady. Only family goes to the back."

Ivy rubbed her hands against her arms as she walked back to Gabe and Lauren. The receptionist acted as if she were nothing to Carter and the children, but she felt as close to them as she did her mother or her sister and her family. She leaned forward and rubbed her temples with both hands as the woman's words echoed through her mind. *Only family goes to the back.*

"Look, Miss Adams, I colored you a picture."

Ivy looked up. She smiled at the page filled with kittens. Lauren called her by her teacher name, her formal name. By all appearances, she was nothing to Carter and his family but a good, Christian woman who helped them when they needed it.

Except she was more than that. She wanted to be. She had to be.

Gabe slammed down his crayon. He furrowed his brows and punched out his lower lip. "I hungry."

Ivy knew he wasn't hungry. The child had eaten a pack-

age of peanut butter crackers, some gummies, and a ba-
nana since she'd gotten here. He was tired and wanted his
bed. He probably needed changed as well.

She picked him up and grabbed his backpack off the
chair. "Lauren, come with me. I'm going to change Gabe's
diaper."

Gabe kicked his legs. "No diaper change."

Ivy ignored his protests as they walked to the bathroom.
She wondered if Carter had tried to start potty training him
yet. Gabe wasn't too many months past three years, but he
was old enough to start trying to use the toilet. Although,
he did act a bit young for his age; so he might not be ready.

Gabe whined and fussed through the process, but Ivy
held firm. She finished changing his diaper then washed
her and his hands. She picked him up and he rubbed his
eyes with the back of his hand. She pressed his head against
her shoulder. "Why don't you rest a minute, little man?"

She expected another battle, but he laid his head against
her and plopped his thumb in his mouth. Reaching up with
his free hand, he twirled a strand of her hair. No matter
what anyone thought, she was family.

Sitting back down, she watched Lauren work a cross-
word puzzle. Gabe succumbed to his exhaustion and rested
heavily on her shoulder. She looked up at the clock on the
wall. Another half hour had passed.

She looked at the receptionist. Ivy knew the woman
probably had plenty of work to get done, but no one had
entered the emergency room in over an hour. *Maybe she'll
go check on him for me.*

Gently standing to her feet as not to wake Gabe, she
made her way back to the receptionist. The woman peered
up at her. "May I help you, miss?"

"It's been two and a half hours, and I'm worried. I just
wondered if you could check on Clay Smith for me."

"Honey, I don't know if you need to be somewhere or if it's that you've gotten stuck taking care of the kids, but you're just gonna have to wait."

Fire surged through Ivy's veins. "Now listen, ma'am—"

The doors opened and Carter and Clay walked out. Clay's face was red and puffy from crying, and his arm was lifted in a sling.

"We're finally done," said Carter.

"You were saying?" The receptionist glared at her.

Ivy swatted her hand in dismissal. "Never mind."

The woman harrumphed, but Ivy ignored her. She looked down at Clay, wishing she could wrap him in a big hug. With Gabe on her shoulder, she couldn't even bend to his level. "How you doing?"

"It hurts." Clay's frown broke her heart.

Carter patted his back. "He was a trooper. They had to set it, and it hurt, didn't it, bud?"

Clay nodded.

"But you did good. Didn't yell one time, did you?"

Clay shook his head.

Lauren spotted them and raced to Clay's side. "Are you okay?"

She tried to hug him, but Carter held her back. "His arm is pretty fragile. We have to go to the doctor when the swelling goes down and get a cast."

Lauren gasped. "You have to have a cast?"

Clay nodded.

He was a boy of few words tonight, and Ivy longed to scoop the child in her arms and kiss away his hurt.

Carter motioned toward the lobby. "Let's get our stuff and get home."

She walked with them to their van and buckled Gabe's seat belt while Carter fixed Clay in his seat. They shut the doors, and Carter walked toward her. "I couldn't have made it through tonight without you."

He stood mere inches in front of her. She reminded herself to continue to breathe. "It was nothing."

"It wasn't nothing."

She looked up at him. He lifted his hand to her cheek then traced it down to her jaw then under her chin. Was he going to kiss her again? She wanted him to. Desperately, she wanted to feel his lips against hers.

No worries about her mother. Or Mary. She wanted to feel his kiss. He leaned down and she sucked in her breath. Stopping at her forehead, he pressed his lips against her then took a step back.

No! She wanted to scream. That wasn't what she wanted. She yearned for more. She wanted to be able to go back to the emergency room. She wanted to be family.

"Thank you, Ivy."

He turned and slid into the van. Numb, she made her way to her car. He waited, as she knew he would, until she'd pulled out of the parking lot.

"God, what am I supposed to do?" She petitioned her Father aloud. "Be strong and courageous?"

The Spirit nudged her. *"Do not be discouraged."*

Sucking in a long breath, she flipped on the radio. A contemporary Christian song about patience through adversity billowed from the speakers. She wasn't sure how much more waiting she could do.

"Which is why you're resting in Me."

"Okay, God." She tapped the steering wheel to the beat of the song. "I'm definitely resting in You."

The doorbell rang, and Carter padded down the hall to answer it. He'd just put Lauren on the bus and taken Gabe to Anna's for the day. Clay had finally gone back to sleep after waking up in pain a few times in the night, and he didn't want whoever it was to wake him. He opened the door. "Ivy?"

She grinned and lifted up a bag. "I brought some chicken noodle soup and lemon-lime soda."

He took in her sweatpants and ponytail. "Aren't you supposed to be at school?"

She shrugged. "I took a sick day so you could go in to work."

"You what?"

Her cheeks blazed as she ducked her chin. "I took a sick day. I thought of it last night, but I figured if I mentioned it to you, you'd say no. And I knew you wouldn't want to take him to a babysitter. And…"

He lifted his finger. "I got it."

"Are you mad?"

"No, I'm not mad." He motioned her inside. "I can't believe you did that, though."

"Why? Carter, I love your kids."

"I know that." But he didn't want her to only love his kids. He wanted to hear her say the words to him. He pointed to the bag. "You do know the boy broke his arm. He doesn't have the flu or a stomach bug."

"I'm well aware of that. I thought the pain medicine might upset his stomach." Ivy stuck out her tongue, and Carter laughed.

"He did have a hard time settling in last night, so you might be right."

She furrowed her brow. "Poor baby. Where is he?"

"In bed."

She nodded as she pulled a pen and pad of paper out of her bag. "Okay. Tell me what time he last took his medicine." She leaned the pen against her lips. "And where do you keep the medicine?"

He bit back a chuckle as he answered all her questions. "You know Lauren's going to be devastated that you're not at school."

She scrunched her nose. "I know. But I'll be here when she gets off the bus. Now you go get ready for work. I'll take care of everything while you're gone."

Carter made his way to his room and changed as she said. But there was no way he was going in to work. He'd already called one of his guys to handle any decisions that needed to be made and to call him if necessary.

He slipped into his coat then walked back down the hall to find her. She stood at the kitchen counter cutting vegetables she must have brought with her. His mind flashed back to more than two years ago. How many times had he watched Mary do the same thing?

For the first time, his heart didn't ache for his deceased wife. He'd loved her completely, but it was time to let her go. Time to bask in Ivy caring for his family. How he wanted to wrap his arms around her and plant a firm kiss to her lips. But he'd have to wait.

"See you later, Ivy."

She waved, and he forced himself out the door. Just to be sure, he called and checked on the jobsite. All was going well. He drove to the grocery and picked up various flavors of doughnuts then made his way to the video store and grabbed a new release. Swinging by the flower shop, he selected a bouquet of red flowers then drove through a froufrou coffee shop to get her some flavored java.

Once back at his house, he balanced all the stuff in his hands. He couldn't wait to see Ivy's face. He rang the doorbell. She pulled open the door, and her jaw dropped. "Carter Smith, what is all this?"

He pushed past her and set the movie, doughnuts, and coffee on the table. He handed the flowers to her. "Ivy, this is probably the closest thing you and I will ever get to a date."

She furrowed her brow. "What?"

"Listen. I'm crazy about you. I know you love my children, and I'm glad you do. 'Cause this would never in a million years work if I didn't think you cared about my kids. But I don't want you just loving them. I want…"

She put the flowers on the end table then placed her index finger on his lips. "Hush."

Before he could respond, she lifted her chin and pressed her lips against his. He wrapped his arms around her and crushed her to his chest. If he had his way, he'd never let her go.

She squeaked. "Can't breathe."

He loosened her just a bit as he kissed the corner of her mouth, her cheek, her nose, then back down to her mouth.

She placed her hands on his chest and pushed him away. Brushing a strand of hair away from her face, she grinned. "Holy cow. Talk about curling a girl's toes." She pointed to his chest. "And by the way, that's just wrong."

He looked down at his shirt. "What?"

She shook her head and blew out a breath. "All those muscles."

He grinned and grabbed her hand, pulling her back to him. "I'll tell you what's wrong." He traced his finger through the length of her hair. "All that beautiful, soft hair." He kissed her eyes, one at a time. "Gorgeous blue eyes."

She wrapped her hands around his neck and kissed his lips again.

He growled. "And your lips are downright painful to me."

She laughed and pulled away from him again. "I hope this means you like me. Not just for the kids' sake."

"I was going to say the same thing to you."

"Carter, I love you."

"I love you, too."

She placed her hands on her chest. "For me. Not just for your kids. Even though I'm not Mary."

Carter grabbed her hand in his and sat her beside him on the couch. "I loved Mary with my whole heart."

Ivy nodded. "I know. Your sincere devotion to her was one of the things that drew me to you."

"I still love Mary, but she's gone. And God brought you to me." He touched her cheek. "I never thought I would love again, but I do."

He kissed her lips again.

"Daddy." Clay's voice sounded from down the hall.

He and Ivy both jumped up.

"I better go check on him."

Carter walked into Clay's room. His son sat up in bed. He looked at the sling as if he were afraid of it. "I'm hungry, Daddy."

Carter helped him up. "Let's get you to the kitchen for something to eat. Miss Adams…" He paused when he said her name. She was so much more than Miss Adams.

"Yeah?" Clay's eyes lit up.

"She's here to see you."

Clay lifted his eyebrows. "She is?"

"Yep. And there're doughnuts in the kitchen if you want one."

Clay finagled his way out of bed and walked down the hall. He smiled at Ivy and waved. "Hi."

She rustled his hair. "How are you doing?"

"Good."

"You hungry?"

"Mmm-hmm."

Carter followed Ivy and Clay into the kitchen. After

eating doughnuts at the table, they walked back into the living room. Clay seemed to be handling the pain well, which meant no alone time with Ivy.

"You wanna watch a movie, son?" He pulled the DVD out of the sack.

Ivy pointed at it and whispered, "Wasn't that supposed to be for us?"

Carter nodded. "Yeah, but it's the latest animated movie release. I figured *us* would include Clay."

Ivy laughed. "Very wise choice."

Chapter 18

Carter could hardly wait to get to the pantry to drop off his and the kids' monthly donation. He looked in the rearview mirror. "Lauren, is it still in the bag?"

He watched as Lauren rolled her eyes. "Daddy, it's not going to go anywhere."

With one hand on the wheel, he smoothed the front of his button-down shirt. He wanted tonight to be perfect. He cocked his head. Well, as perfect as it could be with his girlfriend and three kids under the age of eight.

He pulled into the pantry parking lot, and they all got out of the van. Gabe started to grab bags out of the backseat and Carter stopped him. He found one that Gabe could carry and handed it to his son. Then handed Lauren and Clay the ones he wanted them to carry.

Clay had been out of his cast for only a week, and his arm wasn't quite as strong as the other yet, so Carter gave him a lighter load.

Ivy opened the pantry door and waved them out of the cool air. She hugged each of his children then straightened Gabe's pants so that the zipper was in the front. Potty training had been every bit the challenge Carter feared it would be. But not because of accidents. Rather because the child wanted to use the restroom every five minutes. He was worse than training a puppy. Ivy knelt down to Gabe's eye level. "You gotta go potty?"

Carter rolled his eyes. He didn't want to waste time with bathroom trips. His son had gone just before they left. To his surprise, Gabe shook his head. "No."

Ivy tweaked his nose. "You tell me when you have to go."

She stood up and pulled a ponytail band off her wrist. She made a twirling motion to Lauren. "Okay, turn around."

Carter fought his impatience. "What are you doing?"

"Lauren called and asked me to braid her hair."

Carter threw back his head and stared at the ceiling. His nerves were getting the best of him. His knees trembled. His hands had grown clammy. And he hadn't gotten his hug and kiss yet. And he didn't even want them. He wanted to put the groceries away, as they did every time they dropped food off. The woman was killing him.

He chewed on his bottom lip as he watched Ivy tie knots in Lauren's hair. Finally, she wrapped the ponytail holder around the bottom.

"Can we put away the groceries already?" he asked.

"*May* we?" Ivy said back to him and winked. She looked back at Lauren. "Did you bring the bow?"

Lauren handed her a ribbon, and Carter feared he was going to wring his own daughter's neck. Ivy finished the bow then meandered to him. She kissed his cheek. "Would you stop huffing and puffing over here? The restaurant isn't going anywhere, and you won't die of hunger before we leave."

"He's gonna die if we don't put away these groceries. He's got a…"

Carter nudged Clay's leg with his foot.

Clay squealed. "Hey. That hurt."

Carter fumed. "It did not hurt. I barely touched you."

Ivy motioned them toward the back of the room. "Let's put the groceries away before someone does get hurt."

"Finally," Carter mumbled as he picked up his designated bags and followed her to the back of the building.

"We can't leave until Brent gets back to lock up anyway, so we might as well take our time." She scrunched her nose. "I thought he would have been back by now. He was just running to the bank."

Carter patted his front pocket to be sure he'd remembered the key Brent had given him to use to lock up. He blew out a breath when he felt it. He'd been such a wreck trying to get here, he was surprised he hadn't forgotten.

Gabe handed her his bag, and she stacked the cans of vegetables in their proper places. Lauren handed her another bag. More vegetables. Then a bag with cereal. Some sugar and flour.

Carter's heartbeat sped up as she emptied one grocery bag after another. He wiped his brow with the back of his hand then rubbed his hands together to try to make them less clammy.

"Carter, are you okay? You look a little sick." Ivy stood up and placed the back of her hand against his forehead. "You're kind of sweaty, too."

He pulled her hand away from his face. "I'm fine. Just really hungry."

She furrowed her brow, but didn't say anything else as she took the last bag from his hands. She pulled out a can of tuna then a can of ravioli. Finally, she pulled out the little black box. "What's this?"

"It's a ring!" Clay hollered, and Carter had to fight the urge to flick his son in the back of the head.

Ivy looked up at him. Her eyes shone with love and excitement. She handed the box back to him, and Carter lowered to one knee. "Clay's right. It is a ring."

He waited until Lauren, Clay, and Gabe maneuvered themselves beside him. Each of them wanted a part in presenting the ring to her. Ivy cupped her mouth with her hand, and tears glistened in her eyes.

Carter opened the box and took the solitaire diamond between his fingers. "Ivy, I love you."

"Me, too," said Gabe.

"I do, too," said Clay.

"You know I love you. I loved you first," said Lauren.

"Did not," Clay yelled.

"Did, too."

"Stop it." Carter glared at both of them, and they clamped their mouths shut. He looked back at Ivy, and he could tell she fought back laughter. He raised his eyebrows. "You know it will be like this every day."

She nodded.

"Ivy, will you be my wife?"

Ivy squealed and wrapped her arms around him. She planted a firm, quick kiss to his lips. "Yes."

She kissed Lauren on the forehead. "Yes." Then Clay. "Yes." Then Gabe. "And yes to you, too."

Carter stood and took her hand in his. He slid the ring on her finger. It fit. Her mother had known the right size.

She gazed down at her hand and squealed again. "I can't wait to be your wife." She kissed him again then glanced at each of his children. "And your mommy."

"Does this mean we can call you *Mommy*?" Clay asked.

Ivy looked at him. He could tell she was unsure how to answer. That she worried it would bother him. How could she be concerned? She was their mother. In every sense of the word, except she hadn't given birth to them. If Mary were still alive she would be an excellent mom to the kids. But she was gone, and God had given them another one. Perfect for him and them. Carter patted his son's back. "Of course, you can call her *Mommy*."

Tears filled Ivy's eyes again, and Lauren grabbed her hand. "Does this mean I can call you *Mommy* at school?"

Ivy shrugged. "Well, I don't see why not."

"Do I have to wait until you and Daddy get married to call you *Mommy*?" asked Clay.

Anticipation at making her his wife swelled within him. "You won't have to wait long."

"How long?" asked Clay.

"A week," Carter answered.

Ivy gasped. "How 'bout a month?"

"Really?" Carter's heart beat faster again. "Only a month?"

"I don't want to wait any longer. Do you?"

"No. I don't."

Gabe pulled on Ivy's shirttail, and Carter realized his son held the front of his pants. "Mommy, I gotta go potty."

Ivy stepped onto the sand in her strapless, flowing wedding dress. The warm, December Caribbean sun kissed her cheeks and shoulders. She watched as Lauren walked toward her dad and brothers. No bridesmaids. No groomsmen. Just their family would stand under the white pavilion with the ocean in front of them.

The destination wedding had been a perfect choice for them. Her mother and Phil would enjoy a second honeymoon, though the first one had only been a month ago.

Mirela, Josif, Bella, and Benny would enjoy their first family vacation. And Carter's parents would take the kids for a week of vacation. Ivy grinned. All of them booked to stay three resorts away.

Her mom took Ivy's hand. "Are you ready to do this?"

Ivy reached up and fixed the tropical flower she'd bobby pinned in her hair. "I'm so ready."

Opting for bare feet, something she never thought she'd do, Ivy relished the feel of the sand between her toes as they walked toward Carter and the children.

With the sun shining just above them, Ivy still couldn't make out Carter's face. She hoped he thought her beautiful in the white, satin gown that reached her calves but flowed out with the wind's beckoning. She felt beautiful.

Reaching the steps that led to the pavilion, she could finally see his face. The look of love and pleasure that wrapped his expression squeezed her heart. She tried to walk faster to make it to her groom, but her mom slowed her down. She exhaled a breath to calm her beating heart. How she wanted to be Carter's wife. In every way.

She gazed at the children. Her children. In only a few minutes she would be their mommy, not just in heart or word but legally as well. Everyone would know she *was* family.

Her mom let go of her arm, and Carter took her hand in his. The preacher must have said to do it, but she hadn't heard. All she could think about was making this man her husband and those children her kids.

She gazed up at Carter's face. He mouthed the words *I love you,* and tears welled in her eyes. How she loved this man.

"Do you take this woman to be your lawful wife?"

Carter straightened his shoulders and sucked in a breath. "I do."

And Ivy knew he did. Carter didn't love with just a part of his heart. He threw the whole of himself at a person. Body, mind, and soul. Forever.

A tear streamed down her cheek with thankfulness that God had given her a man who would cherish her all the days of her life. And longer.

Carter reached up and swiped the tear with the back of his hand. His touch sent tingles down her spine.

"Do you take this man to be your lawful husband?"

"I do." And she did. With all that was in her. She took him and his crew. For better or worse. In sickness and health. Till death do they part.

"I now pronounce you man and wife."

Carter cupped her cheeks with both hands and Ivy closed her eyes as he leaned toward her. Her skin burned when his lips touched hers. Not as a boyfriend or a fiancé but as her husband.

She opened her eyes as his lips left hers. He wrapped his arms around her, and Ivy looked over his shoulder at the rolling waves of the crystal clear ocean and the serenity of the cloudless blue sky. God's beauty in nature never ceased to amaze her, to send shivers through her body.

Her husband released her from his embrace. He took her hands in his, and she stared up at him. God's beauty in this man and these kids—her man, her kids—amazed her as well. He had picked the perfect mate for her.

"Now you're officially my mommy," said Lauren.

Clay pointed at his chest. "She was always 'fficially my mommy."

Lauren pushed him. "You don't even know what *officially* means."

"Stop it," growled Carter.

Ivy looked down and noticed Gabe crossed his legs. She grinned as she pointed at their youngest child.

Carter rolled his eyes and motioned to his mother. "Mom, can you come help him?"

"*Will* you…" Ivy corrected him.

Carter squinted at her and Ivy lifted up her palms as she shrugged. "What? I'm a teacher. I can't help myself."

Carter wrapped his arm around her shoulder and planted kisses all over her face. "From now on, every time you correct me, I'm going to waller you in kisses."

Ivy laughed. "Then I'm going to find more ways to correct you."

"Oh yeah?"

"Yeah."

He leaned closer and whispered, "I can't wait until later."

"Me, either."

"You wanna skip out right now?"

Ivy lifted her eyebrows. "Now?"

"Yeah."

She nodded. "Okay."

Carter grinned. "Really?"

Ivy grabbed Clay by the hand. "I'm gonna give the kids a hug first."

Carter raced to his father, Freddie, and whispered something in his ear. His father shook his hand and gave him a quick hug.

Ivy hugged Clay then grabbed Lauren and hugged her as well. "You two have fun this week. Be good for your grandma and grandpa. Now go have fun with Bella."

They ran to their new cousin, and all three of them flopped into the sand and started to build a sandcastle. Ivy pushed away any concerns about ruining new outfits. Today was not a day to worry about germs.

Carter's mother returned with Gabe, and Ivy gave him a quick hug and a kiss on the forehead. She hugged her new mother-in-law as well. "Thanks so much for keeping them, Ruth."

Before his mother could respond, Carter grabbed her by the arm. "We're all set."

"Really?"

"Really. You still want to sneak away?"

Ivy glanced back at Ruth, and the woman winked and motioned for them to get out of there. Ivy grabbed Carter's hand and smiled up at him. "Okay."

They made their way down the stairs and almost to the lobby's patio when Ivy heard Josif. "Where they going?"

"Looks like they're leaving," said Mirela.

"Now?" responded Phil.

"Oh, let them go," said her mother, looping her arms around her new husband's waist.

They walked into the lobby, and Ivy looked up at her new husband. "I'm going to miss the kids something awful this week."

"Me, too, but I'm going to enjoy spending one-on-one time with my wife. Trust me. We'll never have time alone again."

"Promise?"

"Promise."

Ivy laughed as he kissed the top of her head. That was a promise she knew he would keep. And she would cherish every moment as his wife and their mother.

* * * * *

REQUEST YOUR FREE BOOKS!

2 FREE CHRISTIAN NOVELS
PLUS 2
FREE
MYSTERY GIFTS

HEARTSONG
PRESENTS

YES! Please send me 2 Free Heartsong Presents novels and my 2 FREE mystery gifts (gifts are worth about $10). After receiving them, if I don't wish to receive any more books I can return the shipping statement marked "cancel." If I don't cancel, I will receive 4 brand-new novels every month and be billed just $4.24 per book. That's a savings of 20% off the cover price. It's quite a bargain! Shipping and handling is just 50¢ per book in the U.S.* I understand that accepting the 2 free books and gifts places me under no obligation to buy anything. I can always return a shipment and cancel at any time. Even if I never buy another book, the two free books and gifts are mine to keep forever.

159 HDN FT97

Name	(PLEASE PRINT)	
Address		Apt. #
City	State	Zip

Signature (if under 18, a parent or guardian must sign)

Mail to the **Reader Service:**
IN U.S.A.: P.O. Box 1867, Buffalo, NY 14240-1867

Not valid for current subscribers to Heartsong Presents books.

* Terms and prices subject to change without notice. Prices do not include applicable taxes. Sales tax applicable in N.Y. This offer is limited to one order per household. All orders subject to credit approval. Credit or debit balances in a customer's account(s) may be offset by any other outstanding balance owed by or to the customer. Please allow 4 to 6 weeks for delivery. Offer available while quantities last. Offer valid only in the U.S.

Your Privacy—The Reader Service is committed to protecting your privacy. Our Privacy Policy is available online at www.ReaderService.com or upon request from the Reader Service.

We make a portion of our mailing list available to reputable third parties that offer products we believe may interest you. If you prefer that we not exchange your name with third parties, or if you wish to clarify or modify your communication preferences, please visit us at www.ReaderService.com/consumerschoice or write to us at Reader Service Preference Service, P.O. Box 9062, Buffalo, NY 14269. Include your complete name and address.